Madonna in a Fur Coat

Sabahattin Ali (1907–1948) was born in the Ottoman town of Eğridere (now Ardino in southern Bulgaria). A teacher, novelist, short-story writer and journalist, he owned and edited a popular weekly newspaper called *Marko Paşa*. He is admired for the determination with which he defended his political beliefs, which are anchored through his writing. *Madonna in A Fur Coat*, first published in 1943, is his best loved work and a touchstone of Turkish literary culture which continues to resonate profoundly with readers young and old today.

Alexander Dawe has translated several works from French and Turkish including the short stories of Ahmet Hamdi Tanpınar and Sait Faik.

Maureen Freely is a writer, a Professor at Warwick University, and the Chair of Trustees of English PEN. She has published seven novels and numerous translations of twentieth century Turkish classics and contemporary authors including five books by the Nobel Prize-winning novelist Orhan Pamuk.

David Selim Sayers is a founding faculty member of the Paris Institute for Critical Thinking (PICT). He teaches and writes on cultural history, particularly in relation to the Middle East and to narrative arts such as film and literature.

SABAHATTIN ALI

Madonna in a Fur Coat

Translated by Maureen Freely and Alexander Dawe
With an Introduction by David Selim Sayers

PENGUIN BOOKS

PENGUIN CLASSICS

UK | USA | Canada | Ireland | Australia
India | New Zealand | South Africa

Penguin Books is part of the Penguin Random House group of companies
whose addresses can be found at global.penguinrandomhouse.com

First published 1943
This translation first published by Penguin Classics 2016
Published in paperback 2017
001

Text copyright 1943 by Sabahattin Ali
Translation copyright © Maureen Freely and Alexander Dawe, 2016
Introduction copyright © David Selim Sayers, 2021

This book is published by arrangement with ONK Agency, Istanbul, Turkey, 2016

The moral rights of the author and translator have been asserted

Set in 11.25/14 pt Dante MT Std
Typeset by Jouve (UK), Milton Keynes
Printed and bound in Great Britain by Clays Ltd, Elcograf S.p.A.

The authorized representative in the EEA is Penguin Random House Ireland,
Morrison Chambers, 32 Nassau Street, Dublin D02 YH68

A CIP catalogue record for this book is available from the British Library

ISBN: 978-0-241-42226-7

www.greenpenguin.co.uk

MIX
Paper from
responsible sources
FSC
www.fsc.org   FSC® C018179

Penguin Random House is committed to a
sustainable future for our business, our readers
and our planet. This book is made from Forest
Stewardship Council® certified paper.

Introduction

I

'While in Germany, I used to be head over heels for a woman called Frolayn* Puder,' wrote Sabahattin Ali to a female friend in 1933. 'Walking down the street, I'd constantly lose myself in her features rather than watch where I was going. She'd turn to me with a tender smile as if to tell me that she forgave my boorishness. Among all the people I've fallen in love with, none treated me as kindly as this woman. She never even let me catch a scent of her fingertips, but neither did she offend me. She knew exactly how to maintain a constant, never-widening, never-closing distance between us.'

These lines were written seven years before Ali serialized *Madonna in a Fur Coat*, his third and final novel, in the daily newspaper *Hakikat* ('Truth'), where it ran from December 1940 to February 1941. And ever since its publication, much of the debate surrounding *Madonna* has concerned how autobiographical it is. Did Ali really meet a woman named Puder during his studies in Germany? Was she really as tantalizing as she appears in the novel? And did Ali secretly carry a torch for her the rest of his life, even as he, just like his protagonist Raif, got married and became a father?

* Turkified version of the German *Fräulein*, or 'Miss'.

For anyone with more than a passing interest in the life of Sabahattin Ali, such questions can seem annoyingly trivial. In Turkey, after all, Ali is a figure of gravitas. He is among the country's most accomplished authors, his fiction translated and read around the world. He was also an outspoken critic of the Turkish state, a devastatingly incisive observer who harnessed the power of his prose to expose the country's social and political injustices. And finally, he went down in history as a symbol of tragedy, one who paid for the sharpness of his pen and the force of his convictions with his life.

Born in 1907 in an Ottoman province soon to gain independence as Bulgaria, Ali was the eldest son of a military family, his grandfather and father serving as officers in the Ottoman navy and infantry. Ali's father was a progressive thinker who named his two sons after the aristocrat and decentralist politician Prince Sabahaddin and the celebrated poet and atheist Tevfik Fikret, both of whom he counted among his friends. A life of pomp and circumstance, however, was not on the cards for the young Ali as his family's fortunes were reduced by the consecutive shocks of the First World War, the disintegration of the Ottoman Empire, and the foundation of the Turkish Republic. In 1928, not long after completing an education marked by many interruptions, a fair share of disciplinary trouble, and tentative steps towards a literary voice, Ali managed to obtain a scholarship from the Turkish state to study language in Germany, where he stayed until 1930.

Shortly after his return to Istanbul, a twenty-three-year-old Ali walked into the offices of the journal *Resimli Ay* ('Illustrated Month') with the manuscript of a short story in hand. The journal was run by the wife-and-husband-team of Sabiha and Zekeriya Sertel, leftist intellectuals who had encountered the work of thinkers such as Karl Marx and Friedrich Engels while studying in the US in the late 1910s. Upon returning to Turkey, the Sertels became active in journalism and publishing, gathering around them a motley crew of left-leaning youngsters that, in due time, would come to read like a who's who of modern Turkish literature. *Primus inter pares* was the poet Nâzım Hikmet, who had studied in the Soviet Union and was just embarking on the Herculean task of revolutionizing Turkish poetry with the themes of social realism and the aesthetics of free verse.

It was Nâzım Hikmet who took the fledgling author under his wing. He encouraged Ali, who so far had written only short pieces, to try his hand at a novel, and nudged his protégé from romanticism towards realism. Ali's first novel, *Kuyucaklı Yusuf* ('Yusuf from Kuyucak,' 1937), was an unsparing exposé of poverty and exploitation in the Turkish countryside, written in intense consultation with the trailblazing poet and printed by the *Resimli Ay* press. 'Throughout the printing process,' Sabiha Sertel recalls in her memoirs, 'Nâzım stood by the machines and watched. The day the first copy was complete, he brought it to the office in delight and showed it to all of us. The look in his eyes all but proclaimed, "I created this novelist".'

As the thirties went by, the Sertels and their milieu grew into the main progressive opposition to the single-party state that ruled the Republic of Turkey from its establishment in 1923 until after the Second World War. They called attention to the country's wide range of open wounds, from the absence of democracy to a gaping urban–rural divide in opportunity and power. They were persecuted for their troubles, with Ali himself repeatedly serving time for his writings, including in 1932 when he was incarcerated for a poem lampooning the country's ruler, Mustafa Kemal Atatürk. But imprisonment was not the only consequence of Ali's outspokenness. Like most authors past and present, Ali could not live off his writing alone – he depended on teaching and administrative posts in the Turkish bureaucracy. Released from prison after ten months, he found himself blacklisted from state employment and was unable to secure a steady income until 1934, when he published a eulogy to the insulted leader, as grand in its praise as it was modest in quality.

Aspiring to a more stable life, Ali moved to Ankara, re-entered the civil service, and married in 1935, welcoming a baby daughter two years later. He published steadily, including his second novel, *İçimizdeki Şeytan* ('The Devil Within Us'), in 1940. But while his finances improved, the controversies surrounding him continued to sharpen. Many of his writings were banned or provoked intense legal and political debate. Ali reached the peak of his notoriety when he started publishing – with renowned author Aziz Nesin – the satirical political journal *Marko Paşa* in late 1946. As Sertel puts it, 'The alliance of two prodigious forces such as Sabahattin and Aziz Nesin yielded a groundbreaking type of satirical journal . . . *Marko Paşa* became the most successful journal of its day. With a print run of 60,000, it was read in villages, towns, and cities alike.'

The success, however, came at a price. *Marko Paşa* was repeatedly shut down by the authorities, with Ali and Nesin relaunching it under different names such as *Merhum Paşa* ('The Deceased Pasha') and *Malum Paşa* ('The Known Pasha'). The journal lasted about a year, at which point Ali was back in prison, this time for his role as publisher. Upon his release, he once again found himself barred from gainful employment and without any outlet for his writings. Convinced it was only a question of time before he was jailed again, he applied for a passport to leave the country. When his request was denied, he clandestinely attempted to cross the border to Bulgaria. It was during this last adventure that he fell victim to an assassination, still unresolved today but plausibly ascribed to the Turkish state. His family and friends only learned of his death from the papers.

As an author, Ali left an enduring mark on the world of Turkish letters with his myriad non-fiction articles, a treasure trove of short stories and poems, and his three novels. As a person, he was perhaps best remembered for the ceaseless hope, indefatigable passion, and impish sense of humour with which he embraced life. A friend recalled once sighting a rainbow while on a trip with Ali. 'If I ran,' Ali supposedly said, 'do you think I could pass underneath it?' When he passed, he was only forty-one.

2

Unsurprising, then, that *Madonna in a Fur Coat* – along with the romantic rumours around it – has often been dismissed as a slightly vexing footnote in the story of a man of big letters and even bigger ideals. A throwaway trifle, this little book, written perhaps with an eye to the market at a time of personal financial hardship, motivated perhaps by a desire to print something that, for once, wouldn't land its author in court as soon as it appeared. But *Madonna* cannot be wished away that easily. No matter how acclaimed Ali's other work is, and no matter how hotly debated his politics remain, *Madonna in a Fur Coat* is still the Sabahattin Ali novel that everyone reads. What is it, then, that makes this book so popular? Why did Ali write it in the first place? And is it really as worlds apart from the rest of his work as it appears?

Let's start by conceding that *Madonna* truly is among the most autobiographical of Ali's works. Still, the novel's reflection of Ali's life should perhaps be sought less in its romantic details than in its overall themes and progression. In the anonymous narrator and the protagonist Raif, Ali builds not just one, but two alter egos into the novel. Like Ali, both characters are struggling communicators. They are keen observers of humanity, offering piercing and ruthless analyses of others and themselves. They wish to share their observations, the narrator in stories and poems, Raif in paintings and memoirs. And, ultimately, their hopes are frustrated: they are derided by the people around them, the narrator's writings fail to catch on, and Raif abandons his artistic ambitions, choosing to write only for himself.

In terms of age, Sabahattin Ali lands somewhere between his two characters, with Raif playing an older Ali who shares his experience with the younger Ali of the narrator. Indeed, as the novel progresses, Raif and the narrator gradually merge. The narrator becomes obsessed with Raif, replicating his motions, reflecting his behaviours, and even assuming his sickly skin complexion. At one point, Raif and the narrator lock eyes, both weeping as they regard each other, the mirroring between them complete. 'I am just embarking on the journey that you are close to finishing,' the narrator tells Raif. 'I want to understand people. Most of all I want to understand what people did to you.' In the end, the only communication the two characters manage to establish is with each other, giving us a sense of the frustration Ali must have felt in his efforts to stir the hearts and minds of his compatriots.

It is Raif's life story that shows the closest factual parallels to Sabahattin Ali's own. Both the writer and his protagonist are born in the Ottoman Empire at the beginning of the twentieth century. Both enjoy an auspicious start, with Raif the scion of local landlords from the fertile Aegean coast and Ali a military brat with family connections all the way to the palace. Both suffer the destruction of their world as adolescents, coming of age during the First World War, the collapse of the Ottoman

Empire, and the ensuing Turkish–Greek War. Both are partially absent as a new world – the Turkish Republic – replaces the old in the twenties, Raif sent by his father to study the German soap industry, Ali on a state scholarship to study the German language. And both return to the new Turkey with high hopes, just to face alienation, marginalization, and hardship.

But Raif is much more than a mere stand-in for Ali. He is, at the same time, a romantic cliché. Hyper-sensitive in both character and constitution, he is plagued by a Hamlet-like tendency to second-guess himself and a penchant for self-pitying introspection. His love affair with Maria Puder ticks all the boxes of a textbook tragic romance: a capricious and unpredictable love interest; bad omens and portentous daydreams; anxious soul-searching and suicidal thoughts; physical separation and respiratory disease. These conventions of the romantic novel, of course, were not invented by Ali. They were inherited from a list of authors who are duly name-checked in the story and include nineteenth-century greats such as Alexandre Dumas and Victor Hugo from France, Ivan Turgenev from Russia, and Heinrich von Kleist from Germany, the latter among the many authors whom Ali translated into Turkish. And neither did the Turkish interest in romanticism start with Ali. It began in the nineteenth century itself, when Ottoman intellectuals first engaged with Western literature.

It was a heady time in the Ottoman Empire. After centuries of military dominance over their European and Middle Eastern rivals, the Ottomans had started losing ground in the eighteenth century due to Western industrial advancements and colonialist expansion. By the nineteenth century, the empire had entered a process of disintegration, with state coffers empty and many key provinces, including Greece and Egypt, attaining various degrees of independence. It was in this context that a new generation of Ottoman elites – such as Ali's father – turned to the West for models of social and political reform that could give the struggling empire a new lease on life. Part of their efforts was the translation and emulation of Western novels to help European ideas cross over to Ottoman society.

Raif bears a striking resemblance to these late Ottoman intellectuals, plenty of whom spent extended time in the capitals of Europe. Once exposed to Western worldviews, however, many of these would-be reformers found it hard to re-enter the Ottoman mainstream. While their practical skills, such as languages, were highly sought after, their cultural attitudes were frequently regarded as alien or even degenerate, and their intellectual contributions were met with fierce conservative resistance. Often, they found themselves socially isolated, politically exiled, and publicly ridiculed in early Ottoman novels such as Ahmed Midhat's *Felâtun Bey ve Râkım Efendi* (1875) and Recaizade Mahmud Ekrem's *Araba Sevdası* ('A Passion for Carriages', 1898), delightfully vicious send-ups of the Westernized Ottoman dandy.

Despite his weak and desultory pretensions of Turkishness – a modern national identity that does not predate the twentieth century – Raif is an Ottoman at heart, born in the Ottoman Empire, called by an Ottoman patronymic instead of a Turkish family name, and expressing himself in the Arabic letters of the empire rather than the Latin alphabet of the republic. And Raif is not just literally Ottoman. He is also a symbolic manifestation of the empire as 'Sick Man of Europe', caught between past and present, tradition and change, wallowing in romantic hopes of progress and reform while the world prepares to condemn 600 years of Ottoman statehood to the dustbin of history in a mere matter of decades.

Echoing Yakup Kadri Karaosmanoğlu's debut novel *Kiralık*

Konak ('A Mansion for Rent', 1922), Raif's grand but decrepit family mansion represents the Ottoman state, crumbling in its foundations while a nice reception room is maintained to impress the few guests that still bother to drop by. Its inhabitants – Raif's wife, children, and in-laws – stand for the bulk of society, parasitically living off Raif's labours while denying him any meaningful connection. And the failure of Raif's European adventure mirrors the plight of Ottoman modernization, with a Europe that doesn't really want to teach (the German soap-makers' 'company secrets') and an Ottoman who doesn't really want to learn, preferring to chase after pipe dreams rather than submit to the discipline of rigorous training. The novel's symbolic scaffolding is completed by Raif's father, repre-senting the glorious but moribund Ottoman past, and Maria herself, who stands for a Westernized future always more ideal than real.

3

Now, this may all be well and good, but why would Sabahattin Ali choose to pick up this bundle of late Ottoman clichés and recycle it for a novel published in 1940s Turkey? Was he hoping that the familiarity of the genre would attract readers? Or that the established tropes of the genre would protect him against the political controversy of his more daring literary endeavours?

The latter idea seems borne out by the character of Raif, for surely it is hard to imagine a more apolitical protagonist at a more political moment. This moment – the transition from the crumbling Ottoman Empire to the nascent Republic of Turkey – is not only the most storied period in Turkish history, but also the one most thoroughly steeped in narratives of mar-tial heroism, patriotic self-sacrifice, and utopian visions of the future. And while Raif nurses fantasies of himself as a latter-day Mucius Scaevola, the semi-mythical Roman assassin who burned off his own right hand in defiance when captured by Rome's enemies, he himself could not be further removed from even the basics of political awareness, let alone such grand patriotic gestures.

It was this apolitical stance that led Nâzım Hikmet, Ali's literary mentor and political hero, to express his dissatisfaction with Raif's memoirs, that is to say, the bulk of the novel. In a letter written in 1943 from prison, where he had been incarcerated for the previous five years on spurious charges of 'spreading communist propaganda', the great poet told Ali that 'proceeding to the second part, one involuntarily notes what a shame it is that the very original, truly accomplished beginning of the novel, and the opportunities it offered, have been wasted for nothing'.

But what if, to the contrary, the very lack of the political in *Madonna* is one of Ali's boldest political statements? What if Ali's transposition of Ottoman clichés onto modern Turkey was not historical escapism but an oblique way of pointing out that the issues plaguing the empire had been carried over, largely unchallenged, to the republic? And what if Raif is apolitical not because he just can't be bothered, but because he can find nothing in Turkey's 'national struggle of liberation' that inspires him to action?

An intertextual reading seems to support this interpretation. Many late Ottoman authors turned to romantic themes because the stifling censorship under Sultan Abdulhamid II (r. 1876–1909) prevented them from taking up overtly political issues. Ali's choice of a topic and protagonist more at home in the Hamidian era seems to imply that a similar regime of censorship obtained when *Madonna* was written, a verdict confirmed by events such as the 1945 *Tan* raid, in which government-instigated mobs looted the premises of three newspapers, including the Sertels' daily *Tan*, permanently silencing the most effective oppositional publications in the country. State oppression was so palpable that Ali's friends didn't even dare to attend his funeral following his assassination. 'They wanted to lure us out,' Sabiha Sertel writes, 'so they could claim we were staging a communist demonstration at Sabahattin's funeral. Perhaps they would even arrest us all.' In 1950, shortly after being released from prison following a hunger strike, Nâzım Hikmet fled to the Soviet Union to avoid sharing Ali's fate; the Sertels followed him into exile the same year. Neither Nâzım nor Sabiha were ever able to return.

To the attentive reader, Raif's memoirs reverberate with subtle rumblings of discontent. Noting the depreciation his family estate has endured in his absence, Raif tells us that the 'olive groves were of little value. They were offered for even less to buyers wealthy enough to invest in derelict property.' During a visit to Turkey, Raif's former co-lodger Frau Döppke observes that 'I have never seen a country embrace foreigners so warmly.' Scattered throughout the novel, such seemingly innocuous remarks add up to a steady subterranean stream of sociopolitical critique. The young republic's promise of social reform has merely resulted in a redistribution of wealth from dispossessed non-Muslims to a new crony elite. Post-war ideals of national independence have been abandoned to welcome the same foreigners who were plotting to split up the Ottoman Empire in the First World War. And the average person's say in all this has hardly increased from sultan to single party. For Ali and his comrades, voicing such inconvenient truths was not just a matter of politics but one of conscience, and even in a novel as seemingly apolitical as *Madonna*, the same message can be spotted haunting the margins of the romantic narrative.

But Ali is not just critical of modern Turkey; he is equally unsparing in his assessment of 'Europe'. Raif sets out for Weimar Germany in high hopes of finding advanced civilization. He expects to feel at home, to come out of his shell, perhaps even to begin a new life. But these dreams are crushed rather quickly as Europe turns out not to be so different from Turkey after all. 'So this is Europe,' Raif notes drily. 'Why all the fuss?' There is, in fact, quite a lot to fuss about, but hardly in the way Raif had imagined. With the hindsight of 1941, Ali has Raif describe the social degradation and economic destitution of the Weimar Republic, with responses ranging from anti-Semitism to the clamouring for a strongman to make Germany great again. This historical perspective couldn't have been timelier in the early forties, when the Turkish and German states were engaged in heavy flirting and dissenters like Ali were all but shouting from the rooftops to alert their compatriots to the realities of the Nazi regime.

Even here, though, I suspect that the main target of Ali's critique is not Germany but Turkey itself. Many of Raif's observations are equally applicable to both countries, allies in the First World War and faced with similar ordeals in its wake, including political instability and a monstrous wealth gap, manifested in symptoms such as a nihilistic indulgence in sensual hedonism (Ali's Berlin recalls Yakup Kadri's Istanbul in *Sodom ve Gomore* [1928]) and plenty of fruitless dinner conversations about 'how Germany [read Turkey] was to be saved'.

As far as anti-Jewish sentiment is concerned, Raif denies its existence in Turkey, but Ali knows his protagonist is lying. In December 1941, two years before *Madonna* came out as a book, the ship *Struma*, carrying 800 Jewish refugees from Nazi-allied Romania, arrived in Istanbul. Its engine inoperable, the ship was blocked by the Turkish authorities from discharging its passengers and towed back out to the Black Sea, where it was sunk with all hands by a Soviet submarine. And in November 1942, still before *Madonna* appeared in book form, Turkey passed the *Varlık Vergisi* (Wealth Tax), a discriminatory tax on fixed assets that deliberately ruined large parts of the country's remaining Jewish and Christian minorities, forcing many into bankruptcy, others into exile, and those who couldn't pay or flee into detention and labour camps.

The final – and perhaps most unspeakable – parallel Ali implies between Germany and Turkey is, of course, the enthusiastic reception of strongman rulers to right the social ills resulting from agonizingly protracted periods of war and deprivation. While Mustafa Kemal Atatürk, Turkey's original strongman, had already died in 1938, his place was taken by his deputy İsmet İnönü, whose unremarkable stature only made him embrace the strongman-dictator cult all the more wholeheartedly. It was under İnönü that Turkey entered into ever closer collaboration with Nazi Germany, and under his rule that some of the worst atrocities of the Turkish single-party state were committed, including not only the *Struma* incident and the Wealth Tax, but also the incarceration of Nâzım Hikmet, the *Tan* raid, and Sabahattin Ali's murder.

If *Madonna* is not, then, an apolitical novel after all, perhaps Raif's politics need to be reinterpreted from a perspective closer to the twenty-first century than to contemporaries like Nâzım Hikmet. Perhaps Raif does not so much lack a political stance as that he assumes a stance of apathy, a more or less conscious disengagement from the political as the latter becomes dominated by abstract, ominous forces over which the individual seems to lack any reasonable control. And who could fault Raif for being apathetic when Ali's life story seems to teach us that the alternatives were prison, exile, and assassination?

4

This engagement, however oblique, with the topic of political apathy is not the only way in which *Madonna* seems ahead of its time. Especially for the twenty-first-century reader, the novel contains another timely surprise, namely a refreshingly unorthodox dissection of gender. The relationship between Raif and Maria is a complex one, and its complexities place it firmly outside the norms of Western and Turkish societies alike, whether in the twenties, the forties, or today.

It is with a good dose of opprobrium that Raif talks about gender in Berlin, a city he paints as a degenerate, immoral, gender- and age-fluid demimonde. Maria's cabaret performances are at best morally dubious, at worst a mere step from prostitution. At one point, Raif mentions trans sex workers soliciting outside the famous KaDeWe department store, referring to them as 'young men dressed in red boots whose faces were painted like women . . . flashing flirtatious looks at the people passing by'. At another, he describes the 'Romanisches Café', where older women gather at night for the pleasurable company of young gigolos.

But in dismissing these manifestations of gender diversity with a whiff of moral superiority, Raif does protest too much. True, the Ottoman culture from which he hails upheld a strong degree of gender segregation, with flirting a risky endeavour, and with men and women usually finding partners through arranged marriage. Less widely known, however, is the fact that, until the late nineteenth century and its influx of Western ideas, Ottoman society was anything but heteronormative.

Unfettered by the stifling categories of hetero- and homo-sexuality, the sexual practices of many Ottoman subjects could, in today's terms, only be described as fluid. While arranged marriage was the domain of procreative sex, many Ottoman women and men sought pleasure and romance with extramarital partners, strongly preferring same-sex affairs since these carried no particular social stigma and had the added bonus of precluding illegitimate pregnancy. Such affairs were occasional subjects of controversy and criticism, but so widespread overall that even large portions of Ottoman court poetry are devoted to the adoration of a male suitor for his male beloved.

Further complicating the Ottoman gender world, these 'beloveds' were usually adolescents – and especially adolescent boys – who formed a de facto 'third gender' and were regarded as intrinsically desirable by both older men and women. Men in particular could be said to have passed through two genders during their lives, starting with adolescence, in which they were conceived as passive, submissive objects of elders' desires, followed by adulthood, in which they were reframed as active, sexually dominant pursuers. The transition from one stage to the other was not tied to an arbitrary legal age but to marriage and the establishment of one's own household.

When Raif falls in love with Maria – in the most Ottoman way imaginable, by looking at her picture rather than her person – he is right in the middle of this transition. His only adolescent sexual experiences are ones where he describes being taken in hand by older neighbourhood boys – while thrillingly failing to clarify whether the resulting adventures were with women or the boys themselves. He is only just discovering women as objects of desire, as evidenced by his fetishistically intense focus on the appearance and movement of exposed female body parts such as fingers, knees, and lips. And he assumes a submissive role in his relationship with Maria, who brings up his 'femininity' time and again, observing that he is 'so much like . . . a woman. A woman like my mother – you need someone to look after you.'

In stark contrast to this stands Maria's own masculinity. She describes herself as 'like a man' and performs as such in many ways, including certain physical attributes, such as her deep voice, and also certain traditionally male gender roles, such as providing for her feeble mother. Maria even toys with the idea of same-sex attraction: 'Although I know that there is in me no tendency towards the unnatural,' she says, 'I would rather fall in love with a woman.' And it is precisely Raif's non-Western, fluid style of masculinity that attracts Maria; he has none of the 'awful male pride' she routinely endures from the men around her.

And so they meet, and so they love, this man who is more than a man and this woman who is more than a woman, one hailing from a society where heteronormativity hasn't quite caught on yet, the other from a milieu where it is in temporary disarray, slipping through the cracks of geography and history to enjoy a fleeting moment of queer compatibility that is both less and more than friendship, romance or lust. As a scholar whose interests range from folklore to fanfiction, it is not hard for me to imagine twenty-first-century readers recasting Maria and Raif in new incarnations that make Sabahattin Ali's non-binary seeds blossom in the most irreverent ways. I, for one, can't wait to see Maria reborn as a trans woman in an open relationship with her bi best friend Raif.

And while the exploration of such alternative gender constellations must be left to contemporary fans, Maria and Raif at least get as far as exploring alternative definitions of heterosexual togetherness. Having grown up 'far removed from the influences that make most women come to accept their fate', Maria is disgusted by the entitled and expectant attitude of most men towards women. 'Our duties?' she asks sardonically. 'To bow down and obey, and give them whatever they want.' In effect, Maria is talking about a form of white male privilege that has hardly gone out of fashion since the twenties, but one that Raif intuitively circumvents thanks to his non-white cultural background.

They discuss love itself, engaging in open-ended debates to grasp and define its meaning, and finding that for both of them, there can be no love without equality. Maria is looking for 'a man who could sweep me off my feet without resorting to brute strength ... without asking anything of me, without controlling me, or degrading me, a man who could love me and walk by my side ... In other words, a truly powerful man.' Raif echoes this wish: 'I have never thought that I could love someone unless I felt in her the same respect and strength I find in myself.' And while Maria stands by the Western creed that romantic love is completely different from sympathy or affection, Raif contributes the Ottoman-inspired, quasi-pansexual, quasi-polyamorous view that love, ultimately, is love: 'In my opinion, love was not an absolute category. There were many kinds of love, just as there were many ways in which people could show their affection for one another. The name and the shape changed to fit the circumstances.'

Raif and Maria are fumbling towards an authentic relationship that goes beyond gender, ethnicity, or religion (which both of them could care less about), a relationship that seeks the humanity in the other, recognizing the complexities of even the seemingly blandest person, a person like Raif, 'the sort of man who causes us to ask ourselves: "What do they live for? What do they find in life? What logic compels them to keep breathing?" ' This search for humanity, for that which makes us unique and universal at the same time, is what allows *Madonna* to ultimately transcend both the romantic and the political novel and take on the aspect of an existential work more reminiscent of Dostoevsky than of Dumas.

When I first discovered *Madonna* – it was read out to me by my own version of Maria Puder, one I was lucky enough to marry – I would never have thought that this small, unassuming book could continue to reveal new meanings, like a flower blossoming in slow motion, almost a century after its conception. It is this versatility, this continuous opening to surprise and creative re-reading, that makes *Madonna in a Fur Coat* the classic that it is.

David Selim Sayers
Paris Institute for Critical Thinking (PICT)
Paris, France, 31 August 2020

MADONNA IN A FUR COAT

Of all the people I have chanced upon in life, there is no one who has left a greater impression. Months have passed but still Raif Efendi haunts my thoughts. As I sit here alone, I can see his honest face, gazing off into the distance, but ready, nonetheless, to greet all who cross his path with a smile. Yet he was hardly an extraordinary man. Indeed, he was rather ordinary, with no distinguishing features – no different from the hundreds of others we meet and fail to notice in the course of a normal day. Indeed, there was no part of his life – public or private – that might give rise to curiosity. He was, in the end, the sort of man who causes us to ask ourselves: 'What do they live for? What do they find in life? What logic compels them to keep breathing? What philosophy drives them, as they wander the earth?' But we ask in vain, if we fail to look beyond the surface – if we forget that beneath each surface lurks another realm, in which a caged mind whirls alone. It is, perhaps, easier to dismiss a man whose face gives no indication of an inner life. And what a pity that is: a dash of curiosity is all it takes to stumble upon treasures we never expected. That said, we rarely seek that which we do not expect to find. Send a hero into a dragon's den, and his task is clear. It is a hero of another order who can summon up the courage to lower himself into a well of which we have no knowledge. Certainly this was not the case for me; if I came to know Raif Efendi, it was happenstance, pure and simple.

After losing my modest post in a bank – I am still not sure why, they said it was to reduce costs, but within the week they had hired someone else – I spent a long time seeking work in Ankara. My meagre savings kept me going through the summer, but as winter approached, I knew that my days of sleeping on friends' sofas would soon come to an end. My restaurant ration card was to expire within the week, and even this I could not afford to renew. Every failed job application drained me of all hope, even when I knew from the outset that my chances were nil; cut off from my friends, I would go from shop to shop seeking work as a salesman; rejected by them all, I would wander the streets in despair for half the night. From time to time, my friends would invite me over for supper, but even as I sat there, enjoying their food and drink, the fog refused to lift. And here was the strangest thing: the more my situation worsened, the less I could be sure of surviving from one day to the next, the greater my shame and my reluctance to ask for help. I would see a friend in the street – a friend who in the past had been more than willing to suggest where else I might look for work – and I would rush past him, head bowed. I was even different with friends whom I had openly asked for food, or happily borrowed money from. When they asked me how I was doing, I would flash an awkward smile and say, 'Not bad . . . I keep finding bits of work to do, here and there.' With that, I'd take my leave. The more I needed my friends, the more I longed to run away.

One evening, I was ambling along the quiet road between the station and the Exhibition Hall, breathing in the beauties of an Ankara autumn, in the hope that they might lift my heart. The sun reflected in the windows of the People's House had punctured this white marble building with holes the colour of blood; hovering over the pine saplings and the acacia trees was a cloud of smoke that might also have been steam or dust, while a group of bedraggled workers returning from some construction site or another moved in hunchbacked silence over the skid-marked tarmac . . . And everything in this scene seemed content to be where it was. All was well with the world. All was in its proper place. There was, I thought, nothing more I could do. Just then a car sped past me. Glancing at the driver, I thought I recognized him. The car came to a halt a few paces ahead, and the door flew open. Leaning out of the window was my old classmate Hamdi, calling out my name.

I went over to him.

'Where are you off to?' he asked.

'Nowhere. I'm just out for a stroll.'

'Get in, then. Let's go to my house!'

Without waiting for an answer, he ushered me into the seat next to him. Along the way he told me he was on his way home from a tour of a number of factories owned by the firm he now worked for: 'I sent a telegram back to the house to let them know when to expect me. So they'll have the place ready for me. Otherwise I'd never have dared to invite you over!'

I laughed.

Time was when Hamdi and I had seen a great deal of each other, but since losing my job I'd not seen him at all. I knew him to be making a good living as an assistant director of a firm that traded in machinery but also involved itself in forestry and timber. And that was precisely why I had not sought him out after losing my job: I feared that he might think I'd come asking for a loan, not a job.

'Are you still at that bank?' he asked.

'No,' I said, 'I left.'

He looked surprised.

'So where are you working now?'

Half-heartedly, I said, 'I'm unemployed!'

He turned to look me over, taking note of the condition of

my clothes, and then, as if to let me know he did not regret inviting me back to his house, he smiled and gave me a friendly pat on the back. 'Don't worry, we'll talk it over tonight and figure something out!'

He seemed so confident, so pleased with himself. He could now, after all, enjoy the luxury of helping his friends. How I envied him!

His house was small but charming; his wife homely but amiable. Without embarrassment, they kissed each other. Then Hamdi left me to go and wash.

He had not introduced me formally to his wife, so I just stood there in the sitting room, uncertain what to do. Meanwhile, his wife lingered in the doorway, furtively watching me. She seemed to be considering something. Most probably, she was wondering if she should invite me to sit down. Changing her mind, she sidled away.

While I asked myself why it was that Hamdi had left me hanging like this, for I had always known him to be fastidious about such things – if anything, too fastidious – believing, as he did, that attentiveness was a necessary ingredient of success. It was, perhaps, a quirk accorded to those who had risen to positions of importance – to be deliberately inattentive in the presence of old (and less successful) friends. To take on a humble, fatherly tone with friends you have always addressed with some formality, to feel entitled to interrupt them mid-flow with some meaningless question, most often with a soft and compassionate smile . . . I'd had so much of this in recent days that it did not even occur to me to be angry with Hamdi. All I wanted was to put this irksome situation behind me. But at just this moment an old village woman padded in, wearing a head-scarf, a white apron and much-darned black socks, and bearing coffee. So I sat down on one of the armchairs – midnight blue, embroidered in silver – and looked around. On the wall were photographs of relatives and film stars; on the bookshelf that clearly belonged to the wife, there sat a number of cheap novels and fashion magazines. Stacked beneath a side table were a few albums that looked to have been well leafed through by visitors. Not knowing what else to do, I picked up one of them, but before I could open it, Hamdi appeared at the door. He was combing his wet hair with one hand while buttoning up his shirt with the other.

'So, now,' he said. 'Bring me up to date.'

'There's nothing to say, really, beyond what I've already told you.'

He seemed pleased to have run into me. Perhaps because it gave him a chance to show me how well he'd done, or because, when he looked at me, he was so glad he wasn't like me. When misfortune visits those who once walked alongside us, we do tend to feel relief, almost as if we believe we have ourselves been spared, and as we come to convince ourselves that they are suffering in our stead, we feel for these wretched creatures. We feel merciful. This was more or less the tone Hamdi took when he asked, 'Are you still writing?'

'Now and again . . . Some poetry, some stories . . .'

'But tell me, is there ever any profit in such things?'

Again, I laughed. Whereupon he said, 'You really have to stop, my friend!' and went on to lecture me about how, if I wanted to be successful, I had to start being practical, and how empty pursuits like literature could do nothing but harm once your schooldays were behind you. He spoke to me as if I were a child, never considering that I might have something to say, indeed to argue, in response, and he did not shy away from making it clear that it was success that had given him his courage. Meanwhile I just sat there, hiding behind a smile that I was sure must look very foolish, and only served to add to his confidence.

5

'Come and see me tomorrow morning!' he said now. 'We'll see if we can figure something out for you. You have a good brain in that head of yours. You were always pretty lazy, too, but that's not important. Experience is the best teacher! . . . Don't forget now. Get there early.'

He seemed to have forgotten that he himself had been one of the laziest boys in the school. Or else he was taking liberties, knowing that I was not about to challenge him.

As he made to rise from his chair, I jumped up and offered him my hand. 'If you'll excuse me,' I said.

'Why so early, my friend? Oh well, you know best.'

Only then did I remember that he'd invited me to supper. But it seemed to have slipped his mind entirely. I made for the door. As I took my hat, I said: 'Please pass on my respects to your wife!'

'Oh, I shall, I shall. And don't you forget to come in and see me tomorrow! In the meantime, don't be downhearted!' he said, and he patted me on the back.

Darkness had well and truly fallen by the time I left the house. The street lamps were glowing. I took a deep breath. There was dust in the air, but to me it felt wondrously clean and calming. I took my time walking home.

Late the next morning, I went to Hamdi's office – even though I'd had no intention of doing so when leaving his house the previous evening. He had not, after all, made a firm offer. Everyone else I'd asked for help had sent me off with the same trite words: 'Let's see what we can come up with, let's see what we can do.' Nevertheless, I went. It wasn't hope that drove me, so much as the desire to see myself insulted. I was more or less telling myself: 'You sat there in silence last night, and let him play the patron, didn't you? Well then, you're going to see this through to the bitter end, for this is what you deserve.'

The porter took me first to a small waiting room. When I

was ushered into Hamdi's office, I could feel that same foolish smile on my face, and I hated myself even more.

Hamdi was occupied with the stack of papers on his desk, and with the managers rushing in and out of his office. Directed to a chair with a peremptory nod, and lacking the courage to shake his hand, I went to sit down. My confidence had ebbed to the point that I felt as dazed as if he were a real boss, showing me my place, and at the same time I genuinely accepted this treatment as normal. What a great gulf had grown between my old classmate and me since he'd invited me into his car, just over twelve hours ago! How absurd they were, the games we played in the name of friendship; did empty, artificial jockeying of this sort bear any relation whatsoever to the real thing?

Neither Hamdi nor I had changed since yesterday evening. We were who we were. But having discovered a few things about each other, we had allowed these minute details to send us on diverging paths. The strangest thing was that we both accepted this change in our relations, and even found it natural. I felt anger neither at him nor at myself. All I wanted was not to be here.

'I've found you a job!' he announced. Looking straight at me, with those brave, sincere eyes of his, he added, 'I mean, I invented a job. It won't be very taxing. You'll keep track of our dealings with various banks, and especially our own bank . . . You'll be something along the lines of a liaison clerk, coordinating the firm's dealings with banks . . . And when there's nothing else to do, you can see to your own business . . . Write as many poems as you please . . . I've spoken to the director, and we can take you on . . . except that we can't offer you much at the moment: forty or fifty liras. We'll raise your salary later, of course. So let's get going! Success awaits us!'

Without bothering to stand up, he extended his hand. I did the same and thanked him. In his face I could see how thoroughly pleased he was to have been in a position to help me. I thought then that he was not a bad fellow, actually – he had only acted in keeping with his station, and perhaps this had been genuinely necessary. But there was a moment after I left his office when I was not a little tempted to leave this place at once, instead of proceeding to the room he had indicated. But in the end I went shuffling down the corridor, head bowed, asking the first porter I saw if he could show me the way to Raif Efendi's office. He waved at a door and moved on. Again, I stopped. Why couldn't I just leave? Was I incapable of giving up a salary of forty liras? Or was I afraid of having been seen to offend Hamdi? No! I had been out of work for months now. I would leave this place with no prospects, and no idea where to go . . . and stripped of all courage. These were the thoughts that kept me in this dim corridor, waiting for a porter to show me the way.

In the end I peeked through a random door and saw Raif Efendi inside. I'd never met him before. Nevertheless, when I saw this man bowed over his desk, I knew it had to be him. Later, I wondered how I'd made my deduction. Hamdi had said, 'I've arranged for you to have a desk in our German translator Raif Efendi's room. He's a simple man, and a very quiet one, too. Entirely harmless.' At a time when everyone else had moved on to addressing each other as Mr and Mrs, he was still known as Raif Efendi. It was, perhaps, the image conjured up by this description that told me this grey-haired, stubble-faced man with tortoiseshell glasses must be him. I walked in.

He raised his head to look at me with daydreaming eyes, whereupon I said: 'You must be Raif Efendi.'

For a moment he looked me over. Then, in a soft and almost fearful voice, he said: 'Yes. And you must be the new clerk. They just came in now to set up your desk. Welcome! Do come in!'

I went to sit down at my desk. I examined the scratches and faint ink stains on its surface. What I longed to do, as is customary when sitting across from a stranger, was to size him up, and with stolen glances to form my first – and of course, mistaken – impressions. But he, I saw, had no such desire; he just bent down over his work and continued as if I weren't even there.

This continued until noon. By now I was staring at him openly, and without fear. He kept his hair cut short, and it was thinning at the top. The skin between his neck and his small ears was wrinkled. His long, thin fingers wandered from document to document as he conducted his translations without any sign of impatience. From time to time he'd raise his eyes, as if in search of the right word and, when our eyes met, he'd offer me something akin to a smile. Though he looked like an old man when viewed from the side, or from above, he looked enchantingly, and childishly, innocent when he smiled. His clipped blond moustache only added to the effect.

On my way out to eat, I saw him open a desk drawer to pull out a food container and a piece of bread wrapped in paper. 'Bon appétit,' I said, and left the room.

After sitting across from each other in the same room for many long days, we still hadn't spoken much. By now I'd come to know some of the clerks from other departments well enough to go out with them to a coffee house in the evenings to play backgammon. From them I discovered that Raif Efendi was one of the longest-serving clerks in the firm. Before the firm was established, he'd worked as a translator at the bank it now used. No one remembered when he'd started there. It was said that he had a large family to care for and that his salary only just covered his costs. When I asked why the firm had not raised his salary, seeing as he was so senior, and in a firm that was throwing away money, left and right, the young clerks laughed. 'He's a slouch, that's why! We're not even sure how good he really is at languages!' Later on, though, I discovered that his German was excellent, and his translations both accurate and elegant. He could easily translate a letter about sawmill machinery or spare parts, or detailing the qualities of a shipment of ash and pine timber bound from Susak Port in Yugoslavia. When he translated contracts or specifications from Turkish into German, the director sent them off without hesitation. In his free moments he would open his desk drawer to read the book he kept there, never rushing and never removing it from the drawer. So one day I asked, 'What's that, Raif Bey?' He reddened as if I had caught him doing something wrong, and stammered, 'Nothing . . . It's a German novel, that's all!' At once, he closed the drawer. Despite all this, no one in the firm was willing to credit him with mastery of a foreign language. And perhaps not without reason, for there was nothing about the man to suggest he might know one. No foreign word ever crossed his lips. He never spoke about knowing other languages, never carried with him foreign magazines or newspapers. In sum, he bore no resemblance to the sort of man who makes it his life's main business to let the whole world know that he understands French. This was underlined by the fact that he had never asked for his worth to be confirmed with a rise in salary. Nor did he make any effort to seek out other, better-paid work.

He came to work punctually, ate lunch in his room, and in the evening he would pick up a few things at the store and head for home. I invited him to the coffee house a few times, but I couldn't get him to come. 'They're waiting for me at home!' he'd say. So he's a happy family man, I thought, rushing home to his wife and children. Later I discovered that it wasn't like that at all, as I shall chronicle in due course. His long years of hard work did not stop him from being despised at the office.

If our friend Hamdi found the tiniest typographical error in one of Raif Efendi's translations, he'd at once call the poor man in, and sometimes he'd come over to our room to upbraid him. With other clerks he was always more circumspect; knowing that each and every one of them owed their jobs to family connections, he had no wish to cause trouble for himself. If he allowed himself to go red in the face and rail against Raif Efendi in a voice loud enough for the entire building to hear, simply because a translation was a few hours late, it was because he knew the man would never find the courage to stand up to him – that much was easy to see. Can there be any sweeter intoxication than exerting power and authority over one of your own kind? It is, nevertheless, a rare pleasure, to be calculated with care, and enjoyed only with a particular sort of person.

Now and again, Raif Efendi would fall ill and absent himself from the office. Most often it was a common cold that kept him at home. But a long-ago bout of pleurisy had made him exceedingly cautious. A light case of sniffles and he would shut himself away, and when he came out again, he'd be wearing many layers of vests. He'd insist on keeping all the windows in our office shut, and when evening fell, he'd wrap himself in scarves up to his ears, not leaving the office until he'd pulled the collar of his thick, worn coat as high as it would go. But even when he was ill, he did not neglect his work. A messenger would deliver to his home any documents in need of translation and collect them a few hours later. Even so, whenever Hamdi or the director gave him a talking to, they seemed to be saying, 'And don't forget how much mercy we show you, you snivelling child! No matter how often you call in sick, we still keep you on!' They never lost an opportunity to throw it in his face: if the poor man came back after an absence of several days, they would, instead of wishing him well, make barbed remarks:

'So, how's it going? You've knocked this on the head at last, I hope!'

In the meantime, I too had begun to lose patience with Raif Efendi. I did not spend much time at the office. I spent most of my time going with my bag of documents from bank to bank, or to the several government ministries whose orders we'd taken; every now and again, I'd stop by my desk to organize my documents before going through them with the director or his assistant. But even so, I'd come to despair of this tiresome blank of a man who sat so lifelessly across from me, endlessly translating, unless he was reading the German novel he'd tucked away in his drawer. He was, I thought, too timid ever to dare to explore his soul, let alone express it. He had, I thought, no more life inside him than a plant. He rolled in every morning like a machine and did his work, only stopping to read those books of his with needless caution, and then he'd buy a few things at the store and go home. As far as I could see, this numbing routine had, over many years, been interrupted only by his illnesses. According to my new friends, he had lived like this for as long as anyone could remember. No one could remember his ever getting excited about anything. Even in the face of unfounded and uncalled for accusations, he would give his superiors the same calm, blank look; when he asked a secretary to type up a translation, and later, when he thanked her for having done so, he would always do so with the same foolish smile.

One day another translation was late, simply because the typists gave little importance to Raif Efendi's work. Hamdi came into our room, looking very stern: 'How much longer will we have to wait? I told you it was urgent. I told you I was about to leave. But still you haven't translated that letter from the firm in Hungary!'

The other, rising swiftly from his chair, cried: 'I've finished my translation, sir! The ladies just haven't found the time to type it up. They were given other work to do!'

'Didn't I tell you that this letter took priority over everything else?'

'Yes, sir, and I told them that too!'

Again, Hamdi raised his voice: 'Instead of talking back to me, just do your job!' On his way out, he slammed the door.

And Raif Efendi followed him out, to go and plead with the typists once more.

Meanwhile, I thought about Hamdi, who had not graced me with a single glance during his performance. Soon the German translator came back in, to bow his head over his desk once again. As always, his composure astounded and infuriated me. He picked up a pencil and began to scribble something on a sheet of paper. He wasn't writing: he was drawing. But not in the unthinking manner of an angry man. I could see the hint of a self-assured smile beneath that blond moustache, and at the corners of his mouth. His hand was moving swiftly across the page. He kept narrowing his eyes, to look at it more closely. I could tell from that confident smile of his that he was pleased with what he saw. Finally, he put down his pencil, to study it more carefully, while I stared at him, unabashed. For now he was wearing an expression I had never seen before. The sort of expression that people wear only when they are grieving for someone. My surprise made me curious. I couldn't keep still. I was just about to stand up when he rose from his chair, and went off to find the secretaries again. In one leap, I was at his desk, I reached for the page. Then I froze, bewildered.

For here was a sketch, the size of a palm, of Hamdi. In a few masterful lines, he had captured the man's essence. Perhaps someone else would not have seen the resemblance; perhaps, looking at it line by line, the resemblance disappeared, but for someone who had just watched Hamdi hollering in this same room, there was no mistaking him. The mouth was an unspeakably vulgar rectangle, howling with an animal rage. In the eyes – two dashes – I could see both the desire to bore a hole through the object of his fury, and the frustration of failing to do so. The nose, squashed against his cheeks, made him look even more savage ... Yes, this was the man who had stormed into this room only minutes earlier, or rather, this was the likeness of his soul. But this was not what had left me stunned. Since coming to this firm, many months before, I had made a string of judgements about Hamdi. Sometimes I had tried to make excuses for him, but mostly I'd been thinking ill of him. Unable to find the old friend in the man of consequence, I could see neither. But now Raif Efendi had summed him up in just a few well-placed lines, and I could no longer see Hamdi in the same way. Despite his wild and primitive expression, there was something pitiable there too. Nowhere had I seen the line between cruelty and wretchedness so clearly drawn. It was as if I were seeing my friend of ten years for the first time.

At the same time, and in one flash, this drawing explained Raif Efendi to me. For now I could well understand his unwavering serenity and his reluctance to form relationships. For how could a man so intimately acquainted with his surroundings, and so clear and sharp in his observations of others, ever know anger or excitement? What choice did a man like this have, in the face of small-minded attacks, but to stand firm like a rock? Our longings, our disappointments, our fits of rage – we succumb to them when something unexpected happens to us, something that seems to make no sense. Is it even possible to shock a man who is ready for anything, and who knows exactly what to expect from anyone?

Even so, there remained something about Raif Efendi that

troubled me. There were, to my mind, a number of contradictions that the sketch did not explain. The fineness of its execution was anything but amateur. It spoke of long years of practice. There was more here than an eye that could see through to the essence of things. There was also a deft hand that could record that essence in fine and elegant detail.

The door opened. I made to return the sketch to the desk, but I was too late. As Raif Efendi crossed the room with his translation of the letter from the Hungarian firm, I offered my apology: 'It's a lovely sketch.'

I thought he'd be taken by surprise, and be worried that I might give him away. Nothing of the sort. With his usual vague and distant smile, he took the sketch from my hand.

'For a time, many years ago, I was interested in art,' he said. 'Every once in a while, I sketch something, just to keep my hand in . . . silly little things, as you can see . . . just to kill time . . .'

Crumpling up the sketch, he tossed it into the wastepaper basket.

'The secretaries typed this up very fast,' he murmured. 'There are probably some mistakes in it, but if I sit down now to read it through, I'll make Hamdi Bey even angrier . . . And he'd be right . . . Best if I take it to him now.'

With that, he left the room. I followed him with my eyes. 'And he'd be right,' I said under my breath. 'And he'd be right.'

From that day on, I took an intense interest in everything Raif Efendi did, no matter how trivial or absurd. Eager to know more about his true identity, I seized every opportunity to speak to him. He gave no indication of having noticed how much more sociable I'd become. Courteous though he was, he remained, nevertheless, aloof. While on the surface we seemed to be making friends, he never opened himself up to me. Especially after I had met his family, and saw at first hand the duties this family placed on him, I became even more curious about him. The closer I got to him, the more puzzles he threw in my path.

It was during one of his customary illnesses that I made my first visit to his house. Hamdi was about to send off a porter with a letter that needed translating by the next day.

'Give it to me,' I said. 'It will give me a chance to say hello.'

'Good idea ... And while you're there, try and find out what's wrong with him. He's really stretching it this time!'

This had, in fact, been one of his longer spells of sickness. He'd been out of the office for more than a week. One of the porters told me where to go: a house in the İsmetpaşa district. It was the middle of winter. I made my way through the streets as night began to fall, passing through narrow streets whose broken pavements seemed a world away from Ankara's asphalt boulevards. There was one hill, one valley, after another. After a very long walk, having reached what seemed to be the edge of the city, I turned left. Entering a coffee house on the corner, I got directions to the yellow, two-storey house, which stood alone amid empty lots piled high with rocks and sand. I had been told that Raif Efendi lived on the ground floor. I rang the bell. A girl who looked to be about twelve answered the door. When I asked for her father, she pursed her lips and grimaced, somewhat theatrically.

'Come in,' she said.

The inside of the house was not at all what I'd expected. In the hallway that seemed to have been turned into a dining room, there was a large winged table. On the side there was a glass cabinet filled with crystal glassware. On the floor was a fine Sivas carpet. From the kitchen next door, there came the aroma of food. The girl took me into the sitting room. Here, too, the furnishings were fine, even expensive. Red velvet armchairs, low walnut side tables and leaning against the far wall, an enormous radio. Fine cream-coloured lacework adorned every table, and the back of every chair. Hanging from a wall was a plaque in the shape of a ship, on which was written a prayer.

A few minutes later, the girl returned with coffee. She was still wearing that spoiled and mocking smile. When she came again to take my cup, she said, 'My father's not well, sir. He can't get out of bed. He's invited you inside.' As she uttered these words, she seemed to be telling me, if only with her eyes and eyebrows, that I was not worthy of this polite gesture.

I entered the room where Raif Efendi lay in bed – to be shocked again. It bore no resemblance to the rest of the house. This small room looked more like a boarding school dormitory, or a hospital ward, with its row of white beds. A bespectacled Raif Efendi was sitting up in one of them. He struggled to greet me. I looked for a chair. The only two I could see were covered with woollen pullovers, women's stockings and hastily discarded silk dresses. On the side was a puce-coloured wardrobe stuffed with carelessly hung dresses and suits, and knotted bags. The disorder in this room was overwhelming. On a tin tray on the bedside table was a dirty soup bowl that had clearly been sitting there since lunchtime. There was also a jug, sitting alongside a large assortment of medicines, some in bottles, others in tubes.

'Sit down here, my friend!' he said, pointing to the end of his bed.

This I did. He was wearing a brightly coloured women's cardigan with holes at the elbows. His head was resting against the white metal bedstead. His clothes were hanging from the other end.

Seeing me look around the room, the head of the household felt compelled to explain: 'I share this room with the children . . . They make a terrible mess of it . . . It's a small house, after all, we can barely fit into it.'

'Is your family quite big?'

'Big enough! I have one older daughter, studying at the *lycée*. And also the daughter you've seen. And then there's my sister-in-law and her husband, and my two brothers-in-law . . . we live here all together. My sister-in-law has two of her own children. We all know how hard it is to find housing in Ankara. If we lived separately, we'd never manage.

At this point the doorbell began to ring, and from the commotion that ensued, I deduced that some other member of this family had just arrived. After a time, the door opened. In walked a portly woman aged about forty whose short hair fell over her face. She went over to Raif Efendi and whispered something into his ear. Before he could answer, she pointed in my direction.

He introduced us. 'A friend from the office,' he said first. And then, 'My life companion.'

Turning to his wife, he said, 'Take it out of my jacket pocket!'

This time the woman did not lean in to speak. 'I didn't come for money, for goodness' sake! Who is going to go and get the bread? Here you are, still in bed!'

'Send Nurten then. It's only a few minutes' walk.'

'Do you really expect me to send that little child to the store at this hour of the night? It's so cold out there. What's more, she's a girl . . . And anyway, even if I asked her to go, do you think she'd listen?'

Raif Efendi thought for a moment; then he nodded, as if he had found the solution. 'She'll go. She'll go!' he said. Then he resumed his old stare.

After the woman had left the room, he turned to me and

said, 'Even buying bread is a problem in this house. Whenever I fall ill, they can't find anyone else to do it!'

Dutifully, I asked: 'Are your brothers-in-law still young?'

He looked at me without answering. It was almost as if he hadn't heard me. But a few minutes later, he said, 'No, they're not young at all! They both have jobs. They're clerks, like us. My brother-in-law's sister set them up at the Ministry of Economic Affairs. They never completed their studies. Not so much as a middle school diploma between them!'

Stopping short, he asked: 'Did you bring me something to translate?'

'Yes, they need it by tomorrow. They'll be sending a porter to collect it tomorrow morning.'

He took the documents and put them to one side.

'And I'm worried about this illness of yours.'

'Thank you . . . It's gone on a long time. I don't dare get up!'

There was a strange light in his eyes. As if he were trying to figure out if he still held my interest. I was ready to go to any lengths to convince him that he did, for this was the first time I had seen the slightest flash of passion in the man. But in no time he had resumed his old blank expression, his old empty smile.

With a sigh, I rose.

And suddenly, he sat up straight and took my hand. 'Thank you so much for coming, my son!'

There was warmth in his voice. It was almost as if he understood how I felt.

Indeed, it was after this visit that we began to draw closer. I wouldn't go so far as to say he treated me differently. It would never even cross my mind to say he was comfortable in my company, or that he began to open up. He was the same quiet, withdrawn man he'd always been. There were, in fact, evenings when we left the office together, and walked as far as his house. Sometimes I'd go inside with him, and drink coffee in the sitting room with the red chairs. But on those occasions, we would talk only about trivial matters – how expensive it was to live in Ankara, and how bad the pavements were in İsmetpaşa district. Only rarely did he mention anything about the family, or the children. From time to time, he'd say, 'My daughter got a bad mark in arithmetic again!' before moving on to another subject. I didn't feel I could ask him to explain more. I had not, after all, formed a very favourable impression of his family on that first visit.

After leaving the patient, I'd passed through the hallway, where two boys aged fifteen or sixteen were in a huddle with a girl of about the same age, and without waiting for me to turn my back, they began whispering and giggling. I knew there was nothing about my appearance to laugh about. But like the empty-headed teenagers they were, they made themselves feel important by laughing at anyone who happened to pass. Even little Nurten had to struggle to be accepted. During my subsequent visits, I saw more of the same. I was myself a young man, still in my twenty-fifth year, but I was constantly being brought up short by this new habit among people my age and younger: seeing a stranger for the first time, they'd look at him with blatant curiosity, as if they had never seen anything like him. It was clear to me that Raif Efendi's domestic situation was not at all pleasant: they treated him as if he were expendable, and always in the way.

Later, when I'd been coming and going for some time, I got to know these children better. And they weren't bad people at all. Rather, they had nothing, absolutely nothing, inside. All their impertinences came from that. It was the yawning void inside them that drove them to deride, scorn and ridicule others, for this was their only source of satisfaction, their only way of knowing who they were. I'd listen to the way they talked to each other. Vedat and Cihat were the youngest clerks in the Ministry of Economic Affairs, but all they ever did was to run down everyone they worked with. When Raif Efendi's older daughter, Necla, spoke, it was only to criticize her classmates. They were forever ridiculing others for the way they walked or the way they dressed, even though they themselves did much the same.

'Did you see what Mualla wore to that wedding? Ha ha ha . . .'

'You should have seen how that girl snubbed our Orhan. Ha ha ha.'

Meanwhile, Raif Efendi's sister-in-law Ferhunde Hanım had no other aim in life than to care for her two children, aged three and four, and (if she could get her older sister to babysit) to put on a lot of make-up, throw on a silk dress and head out for the evening. The few times I saw her, she was standing in front of the mirror of the cabinet in the dining room, fixing a feathered hat over her wavy dyed hair. She could not have been more than thirty years old, but already there were wrinkles around her mouth and her eyes. Her restless baby-blue eyes reflected an inner turmoil that must have been with her since birth. Her children were always wan, unkempt and dirty, and she'd rail against them as if they were a punishment visited on her by a vicious enemy, despairing that they might put their soiled hands on her finery before she went out.

As for Ferhunde's husband, Nurettin Bey, who served as one of the directors at the same branch of the Ministry of Economic Affairs – he was another version of Hamdi. Still in his early thirties, he was the sort of man who puffed up like a barber's assistant when he combed back his dark curly hair, and who, if he said so much as a simple 'How are you?', nodded as if he had just dispensed a rare pearl of wisdom. When someone spoke to him, he'd fix his eyes on him and smile as if to say, 'What sort of nonsense is this, then? As if you knew what you were talking about.'

After finishing vocational college, he'd been sent to Italy, for some reason, to learn more about the leather trade, but all he'd learned while there was a smattering of Italian and the affectations befitting a man of importance. To this he had added his own ideas about how to be successful in life. First, he saw himself as deserving of high rank, and therefore in a position to make half-baked pronouncements at every turn, no matter how little he actually knew about the matter at hand. By criticizing everyone else at the same time, he succeeded in convincing them of his importance. (By my reckoning, the children of the house had acquired this same habit from their uncle, whom they hugely admired.) Secondly, he dressed with great care, shaving every day, making sure his thinning trousers were perfectly ironed, and devoting his Saturdays to long shopping excursions in search of the most fashionable shoes for himself, and the most divine socks. As I later discovered, all his wages went on his and his wife's clothes. The two brothers-in-law, meanwhile, earned no more than thirty-five liras apiece, which meant that it fell to our friend Raif Efendi to cover all the household expenses with his meagre salary. Even so, apart from the poor old man, Nurettin Bey treated every member of the household like a servant. They took the same view of Raif's wife, Mihriye Hanım. Though not yet forty, she was already old, fat and misshapen, with breasts that hung down to her navel. She spent most of her day cooking in the kitchen, devoting any free time that remained to darning pile after pile of children's socks, or caring for her sister's 'brats'. She had no help from the others, who believed that they deserved far better than she could provide; when the food was not to their liking, there were unpleasant scenes. So when Nurettin Bey said, 'What is this meant to be, my dear?' there was as much indignation in his voice as one might expect if he'd contributed many hundreds of liras to the household budget. And the two brothers-in-law would sit there in their seven-lira cravats and say, 'I don't like this, go and make me some eggs!' Or, 'I'm still hungry, go make me some sausages!' They had no qualms about sending Mihriye Hanım back to the kitchen, and if ever they needed eleven kuruş for bread of an evening, instead of reaching into their own pockets, they would go and find Raif Efendi in his sickbed and wake him up, and as if that were not enough, they'd get angry at him for having failed to recover in time to go to the store in their place.

Though the parts of the house that guests rarely saw were a shambles, the hallway and the sitting room were perfectly arranged, and this was Necla's doing. And the others succeeded in maintaining this illusion, even when their friends came to visit.

So they had all joined together to pay for furniture on instalment, squeezing their resources even further. But now they had a red velvet suite that made their guests swoon in admiration, and a twelve-valve radio that was loud enough for the entire neighbourhood to hear. There was also the set of gold-gilded crystal in the glass cabinet, which greatly impressed Nurettin Bey's friends on the many occasions when he invited them over to drink rakı.

Though it was Raif Efendi who bore the cost of all this, it made no difference to him if he was present or absent. Everyone in the family, from the oldest to the youngest, regarded him as irrelevant. They spoke to him about their daily needs and money problems, and nothing else. Mostly, they preferred Mihriye Hanım to be their interlocutor. They sent him off like some sort of lifeless robot in the morning with a list of things to buy, and in the evening he would come back with his arms full. Five years earlier, while courting Fernunde Hanım, Nurettin Bey had been most attentive to Raif Efendi, playing the perfect suitor and never forgetting to bring something to please his prospective brother-in-law every time he came to visit, but now he acted as if it were an insult to have to share a house with a man of so little consequence. They resented him for failing to earn more money, so as to provide the luxuries they craved, but at the same time they regarded him as a man of no value – a nonentity. Encouraged, perhaps, by their elders, even Necla, who seemed to have a head on her shoulders, and Nurten, still in primary school, seemed to share this view. Whatever affection they showed him was rushed and brushed away, like a tedious chore; when he fell ill, they affected the sort of false compassion that one might show to a beggar. Ground down though Mihriye Hanım was by the thankless and never-ending struggle to make ends meet, only she gave him the time of day, doing what she could to ensure that his own children did not belittle or despise him.

On evenings when there were guests, she would pull her husband into the bedroom and, fearing that Nurettin Bey or one of her brothers might suddenly shout out, 'Let's send my uncle out for supplies!', she would put on a sweet voice and say, 'Why don't you slip out and buy us eight eggs and a bottle of rakı? Let's not make them get up from the table.' But never did she ask herself why she and her husband were not sitting at that table, or why, on the rare occasions that they did join the party, they were treated with such disrespect – though perhaps she didn't even notice.

Raif Efendi treated her with an odd sort of tenderness. It was almost as if he pitied this woman who could go for months without taking off her housecoat. From time to time, he'd ask: 'How are you, my wife, has the day been very tiring?'

And sometimes he would take her to one side to talk about

how the children were doing in school, and how to cover the costs of an impending religious holiday.

But he gave no sign of being attached to any other member of their household. Sometimes he would gaze at his older daughter, as if expecting her to say something to him, something sweet and warm. But these moments would pass quickly, as if the girl had, with a needless wiggle, reminded him of the gulf between them.

I thought a great deal about all this. It seemed impossible that a man like Raif Efendi – what sort of man that might be, I too had no idea, but I was sure he was not as he seemed – that a man like this would willingly shrink away from those closest to him. It was more that he did not wish those around him to know who he was, and he was not, in any event, the sort of man who would be willing to exert himself to be known. There was no chance that the ice might melt, to allay the terrible estrangement that divided them. Rather than embark on the arduous task of getting to know each other, they preferred to wander about blindly, noticing each other's presence only when they happened to collide.

But as I mentioned earlier, Raif Efendi did seem to expect something from his older daughter, Necla. As slavishly as she copied the mannerisms of her heavily rouged aunt, as willing as she was to take spiritual guidance from her uncle, there seemed, nevertheless, to be the remnants of a genuine person hiding inside that thick shell of hers. When she scolded her sister, Nurten, for disrespecting their father, there was, at times, a note of indignation. If, at the table or in the bedroom, the others ridiculed Raif Efendi too harshly, she would leave in a huff, slamming the door behind her. But she did so simply to give the genuine person inside her a chance to breathe now and then. Her false self, patiently nurtured over many years, was strong enough to keep her true identity suppressed.

But – and perhaps this was down to the impatience of youth – Raif Efendi's formidable silence in the face of all this made me angry. At home and at the office, he did more than just tolerate ridicule from people with whom he had nothing in common: he seemed actively to approve of those who looked down on him –I knew full well that people who feel misunderstood and misjudged by those around them come to take pride in their plight, finding bitter pleasure in it, but I'd never imagined that they might also come to approve of those who did them down.

I had, on many occasions, seen that he was not a man who blunted his feelings. On the contrary, I knew him to be watchful, attentive to detail and easily offended. He looked at things squarely, missing nothing. Once, when he heard his daughters bickering over who was to bring me coffee, he said nothing, but ten days later, when I returned to his house, he'd called out to them, saying: 'Don't make him coffee! He doesn't want any!'

In fending off a repeat of the incident, he let me know how much it had upset him. He thereby opened himself up to me, and from then on I felt much closer.

Still our conversations remained superficial. But this no longer puzzled me. For wasn't there sufficient pleasure to be had in silent patience – in viewing others' vices with compassion and enjoying their vulgarities? When we walked side by side, did I not feel his humanity most profoundly? Only now did I begin to understand why it was not always through words that people sought each other out and came to understand each other, and why some poets went to such lengths to seek out companions who could, like them, contemplate the beauties of nature in silence. Though I did not know what I was learning from this silent man walking alongside me, I was certain that I was learning far more than I would have done from a teacher of many years.

And I believed he liked me. He was no longer timid and tentative, as he was with all others, and had been with me when we'd first met. Though there were days when some sort of wildness manifested itself: his eyes would narrow, losing all expression, and when addressed, he would answer carefully, but in a voice that made it clear he was not to be approached. On days like this, he would neglect even his translation. Instead, he would sit there for hours, staring at the pile of papers in front of him. It was almost as if he had withdrawn to another time – a place that was his and his alone – and nothing I could do would bring him back. But I would fill with dread, for strange as it might sound, it was generally after these episodes that Raif Efendi would fall ill. I was soon to find out why, in a very sad way.

One day in mid February, Raif Efendi didn't turn up at the office. When I turned up at the house that evening, Mihriye Hanım opened the door.

'Is it you?' she said. 'Oh, do come in. He's just drifted off to sleep . . . but if you like, I can wake him up.'

'No, please don't,' I said. 'I wouldn't want to disturb him. How is he?'

'He's running a fever. And he's complaining of a stomach ache this time, too.' Then, in a complaining voice, she added: 'He just doesn't look after himself, poor man . . . he's not a child anymore. He loses his temper over nothing . . . I have no idea why . . . he won't talk to anyone . . . he wanders out into the streets . . . then becomes ill again . . . and then he retreats to his bed.'

Just then, we could hear Raif Efendi calling from the next room. The woman rushed straight in. I had no idea what to make of what she'd said. Here was a man who guarded his health most jealously, who wrapped himself up in layer after layer of woollen vests and pullovers – how could he ever be capable of the slightest imprudence?

Mihriye Hanım came back into the room. 'The doorbell woke him up. Do come in!'

On this occasion Raif Efendi seemed thoroughly dejected. His complexion was yellow, and his breathing rapid. His customary childish smile struck me more as a grin needlessly stretching his facial muscles. Behind his glasses, his eyes seemed more distant than ever.

'So what's happened to you, Raif Bey? We hope you'll get over it soon.'

'Thank you!'

His voice was a bit hoarse. When he coughed, his chest rattled and shook.

To allay my curiosity as fast as I could, I asked: 'How did you come down with this cold? By letting yourself get a chill, I imagine.'

For a long time he just stared at the white sheets on his bed. The little iron stove that his wife and children had squeezed between the beds had made the room too hot. In spite of this, the man still looked cold. Pulling his blankets up to his chin, he said: 'Yes, I let myself catch a chill. Last night after supper, I went outside for a while . . .'

'Did you go somewhere?'

'No. I just wanted to take a little walk. Why, I don't know. I was upset, maybe.'

It surprised me to hear him admit to being upset.

'I walked a little too far. As far as the Agricultural Institute. To the foot of Keçiören Hill. Was I walking very fast? I just don't know. I felt hot. I opened up my coat. It was a windy night. And snowing a little, too. I probably caught a chill.'

Walking down deserted streets for hours in the night, through wind and snow, opening up his chest to the cold – this was not something I would have expected from Raif Efendi.

'Were you upset about something?' I asked.

He answered in a rush: 'Not at all, my dear friend. It just happens like this, from time to time. I suddenly get the urge to walk through the night. Who knows? Maybe it's the noise in the house that drives me out!'

And then, as if fearing he might have said too much: 'Sometimes people do such things, as they get on in years. How could we ever blame the young ones?'

Once again, I could hear noise outside and whispering. The older girl had just come home from school, and she came in to kiss her father's cheeks.

'How are you feeling, dear father?'

Then she turned around and took my hand: 'This happens all the time, sir ... Every once in a while, an idea flashes through his mind, and he says he's off to the coffee house, and then, it might be in the coffee house that he catches a chill, or it might be on his way home, but he falls ill ... I've lost count of the times ... I have no idea what is going on in that coffee house!'

Taking off her coat and tossing it onto a chair, she left the room. Raif Efendi looked as if he were used to such behaviour and didn't consider it very important.

I looked at the patient's face. He had turned to look at me, and in those eyes I saw no light, no surprise. I was less interested in knowing why he had lied to his family than in knowing why he had told me the truth, but I also took pride in it: the pride of being closer to someone than others.

After leaving the house to make my way home, I let my thoughts wander. What if Raif Efendi really were a simple man with nothing inside? It was clear that he had no purpose, no passion, no connection to others, not even those who were closest to him ... So what did he want from life? Was it perhaps this emptiness inside – this lack of purpose – that sent him out to roam the streets by night?

29

At this point, I saw that I had reached the hotel where I was living. The small room I was sharing with a friend there was only just big enough to fit in two beds. It was just gone eight o'clock. I wasn't feeling hungry so I thought I might go up to my room and read for a while, but I soon rejected the idea, for this was the time of night when the coffee house on the ground floor turned its gramophone up to top volume, and the Syrian nightclub performer who lived in the next room would sing shrilly in Arabic while dressing for work. So I turned around and walked down the muddy asphalt in the direction of Keçiören. At first there were only car repair shops and ramshackle coffee houses lining the road. Then, to the right, there were houses on the rising hillside; in the hollow to the left there were gardens lined with leafless trees. I raised up my collar. The wind was harsh and wet. I was swept up by a wild urge that usually only came to me when I was drunk: to keep on walking, to run. I felt as if I could go on like this for hours, or even days. I lost track of where I was. I had gone a long way. The wind was even stronger now, and it pushed against my chest; and it gave me pleasure to have to battle with it to keep advancing.

Then suddenly I wondered why I was here . . . For nothing . . . there was no reason. I'd made no decision to come here, I'd just started walking. The trees on either side of the road were wailing with the wind, and the clouds were racing overhead. The dark cliffs in the hills above were still visible, and the clouds heading towards them seemed each to leave a part of itself behind. Shutting my eyes, I breathed in the moist air. And once again I asked myself: why have I come here? The wind was much the same as it had been the night before, and perhaps there would be a snow flurry . . . The night before, it had been another man in these parts, his glasses fogging up, his hat in his hand, and his shirt open, walking and breaking into a run . . .

The wind was cutting through his thin, cropped hair, and who could say how much it cooled his overheated head? What was inside that head of his? What had brought that head, that invalid, that ageing body, to these parts? I wanted to imagine Raif Bey walking through that dark, cold night, I wanted to see how his face changed shape. And now I understand what had driven me here: being here might help me understand him, might help me see inside his head. But all I could see was the wind tugging at my hat, and the wailing trees, and the clouds changing shape as they raced across the sky. To live in the same places was not to live as he did. To assume such a thing might be possible, you had to be as brash and naive as I was.

I raced back to the hotel. The coffee-house gramophone was no longer playing, and the Syrian woman no longer singing. My friend was lying in bed, reading a book. He threw me a glance. 'What's up? Back from a night of debauchery, are you?'

How easily people can read each other! . . . And there I was, trying so hard to penetrate someone else's mind, to find out if the soul hiding inside it was ordered or in turmoil. For even the most wretched and simple-minded man could be a surprise, even a fool could have a soul whose torments were a constant source of amazement. Why are we so slow to see this, and why do we assume that it is the easiest thing in the world to know and judge another? Why, when we are reluctant even to describe a wedge of cheese we are seeing for the first time, do we draw our final conclusions from our first encounters with people, and happily dismiss them?

For a long time I couldn't get to sleep. I kept thinking of Raif Efendi, feverish inside his white sheets, in a room thick with the scent of his daughters' young bodies and his wife's tired limbs. His eyes were closed, and who could say where his soul was roaming?

This time Raif Efendi's illness lasted a long time. It was more than his usual cold. The doctor Nurettin Bey called in prescribed mustard paste and cough syrup. I dropped by once every two or three days, and each time his condition seemed to have worsened. But this didn't seem to worry him. He just shrugged it off. Perhaps this was to avoid upsetting his family. But it was the opposite with Mihriye Hanım and Necla. Their behaviour was most disquieting. His wife's long years of drudgery seemed to have robbed the woman of the ability to think: she wandered in a daze from room to room, dropping towels and plates as she rubbed mustard paste on his back; she was always misplacing things and walking around in circles looking for them. I can still see her racing in all directions, her bare feet rippling out of her flat, bent slippers. I can still feel her beseeching eyes on me. Necla was as bereft, and as desperately lost, as her mother. She was staying home from school to sit with her father. When I came to see the patient in the evening, I could tell from her red, swollen eyes that she had been crying. But Raif Bey seemed to find all this annoying. If ever we were left alone, he'd complain about it. Once he even said: 'Honestly! What's going on with these two? Am I on the brink of death? And what if I did die? What would they care? What am I to them?'

Later, in a voice that was even more pained, even more cruel, he added: 'I'm nothing to them ... and I never have been. For years, we've lived in the same house ... never once did they ask themselves who this man was they shared their life with ... and now they're worried I'm going to leave them ...'

'Raif Bey! Please!' I cried. 'What are you saying? Yes, they do seem unusually anxious, but it's not right to talk like that about your wife and your daughter!'

'Yes. They're my wife and my daughter. But nothing more ...'

He turned his head away. Mystified by his last words, I dared not ask a thing.

To bring calm to the family, Nurettin Bey called in an expert in internal medicine. After a long examination, this man diagnosed pneumonia and, seeing the shock he had caused, he said: 'Look here, my dear people. It's nothing serious. He has a strong constitution and a heart in good working condition. He'll come out of it. There's just one thing he has to watch out for. He mustn't catch a chill. It would be better if you took him to hospital!'

Hearing the word hospital, Mihriye Hanım lost control of herself. Collapsing into one of the chairs in the hallway, she began to sob. While Nurettin Bey screwed up his face, as if his pride had been piqued. 'Where's the logic in that?' he said. 'He's likely to get better care at home than in a hospital!'

The doctor shrugged his shoulders and left.

At first Raif Efendi was in favour of going into hospital, saying: 'At least there I might be able to hear myself think!' It was clear that he wanted to be alone, but when he saw how much the others were set against it, he gave up. Smiling hopelessly, he murmured, 'They wouldn't leave me in peace there either!'

One day in particular stays with me. It was a Friday evening, and I was sitting on a chair next to Raif Efendi, saying nothing and watching his wheezing chest. There was no one else in the room. A large pocket watch sitting among the medicines on his bedside table filled the room with its metallic ticking. Opening his sunken eyes, the patient said: 'I'm feeling a little better today!'

'Of course you are. It was never going to go on like this for ever . . .'

Whereupon, in an aggrieved voice, he said: 'Fine, but how much longer *will* this go on?'

Catching his true meaning, I was filled with dread. The weariness in his voice left me in no doubt as to what he meant.

'Please, Raif Bey, can you tell me what's happened?' I asked.

Looking straight into my eyes, he said: 'Fine then. But what's the point? Isn't this enough?'

At this point Mihriye Hanım came into the room. Coming over to me, she said: 'He's feeling better today! It looks like he's going to pull through, thank God!'

Then she turned to her husband. 'We're sending out the washing. Could you ask this gentleman to bring back your towel?'

Raif Efendi nodded in good time. After going through a few drawers, the woman left the room. The slightest improvement in the patient had chased away all her worries. Now she was her old self, busy with housework, cooking and laundry. Like all simple people, she could go in an instant from sorrow to happiness, and excitement to calm, and like all women she forgot things quickly.

In Raif Efendi's eyes, I could see a deep and sorrowful smile. Nodding at the jacket hanging from the foot of his bed, he said: 'In the right-hand pocket, you'll find a key. Take it with you, and open up the top drawer in my desk. And bring back the towel my wife just asked for . . . It's a lot to ask, but . . .'

'I'll bring it tomorrow morning!'

Fixing his eyes on the ceiling, he was silent for a time. Then suddenly he turned towards me. 'Bring me everything you find in that drawer! Whatever you find there . . . My wife seems to know that I'm never going back to that office. I'm bound for other parts . . .'

With that, he buried his face in his pillow.

The next day, before leaving the office, I went over to Raif Efendi's desk. There were three drawers, on the right-hand side. First I opened the two on the bottom. One was empty, and the other was full of papers and rough translations. Putting the key into the lock of the top drawer, a chill went through me. For now I realized I was sitting in the chair that Raif Efendi had occupied for many long years, and doing something he himself had done several times each day. Quickly, I opened the drawer. It was almost empty. Nothing but a dirty-looking towel, a bar of soap wrapped up in newspaper, the lid of a food container, a fork and a threaded Singer pen-knife. I wrapped these up quickly. I stood up and closed the drawer, but at that moment I thought I should make sure there wasn't anything else in there, so I opened it up again and reached into the back. And there, in the drawer's furthest reaches, was something that felt like a notebook. I tossed that in with the rest of it and hurried away. I couldn't stop thinking that Raif Efendi might never sit in that chair, or open that drawer, again.

Arriving at the house, I found the household in turmoil. It was Necla who opened the door, and when she saw me she shook her head and said, 'Don't even ask!' I had become one of the family by now, and no one thought to treat me like a stranger. The young girl said: 'My father's taken a turn for the worse again! Actually, he had two bad turns today. My uncle called the doctor, and he's in there with him now . . . giving him an injection . . .' With that, she ran off into the sickroom.

I did not follow her inside. Instead I sat down on one of the chairs in the hallway, with my package sitting before me. Though Mihriye Hanım came out a few times, I felt too ashamed to hand the sorry thing over to her. Inside that room a man was fighting for his life, and it didn't seem right for me to give any member of his family a dirty towel and an old fork. So I stood up and began pacing around the big table. Glancing into the mirror above the glass cabinet, I was given another shock. I looked jaundiced. My heart began to pound.

The struggle across the great bridge between life and death was a terrifying thing indeed. With his wife, his daughters and his relatives gathered around him, it seemed to me that I had no right to show more sorrow and attachment than they.

Just then my eye was drawn to a crack in the door to the sitting room. Moving closer, I saw Raif Efendi's brothers-in-law Vedat and Cihat. They were sitting side by side on a sofa, smoking. They were thoroughly put out, these two: clearly frustrated at being confined to the house, they had banded together. Nurten was sitting in an armchair, her head resting on her arms: crying, or perhaps sleeping. Some way away, Raif Efendi's sister-in law Ferhunde was sitting with her two children on her lap, trying to stop them making too much noise, but every word she uttered and everything she did showed what a novice she was when it came to consoling a child.

The door to the sickroom opened and out came the doctor with Nurettin behind him. For all his nonchalance, he still looked disgruntled.

'Don't leave his side,' said the doctor. 'And if he has another seizure, give him one of those injections.'

Nurettin Bey frowned. 'Is he in danger?'

The doctor said what all doctors say in such circumstances. 'It's hard to say.'

To avoid further questions, and, even more, to save himself from being harassed by the invalid's wife, he quickly donned his coat and hat; taking the three silver liras from Nurettin Bey, he grimaced and left the house.

Slowly I approached the sickroom door. I peered inside. Mihriye Hanım and Necla were standing over Raif Efendi, watching him with apprehension. He had his eyes closed. When the young girl caught sight of me, she beckoned me over. What both she and her mother wanted, it seemed, was to see how I responded when I saw my friend. Seeing that, I did everything in my power to keep myself under control. I nodded affably, as if I were fine with what I saw. Then I turned to my left. There they were, huddled together. I forced a smile. 'There's nothing to fear, most probably. With God's help, he'll pull through.'

My friend opened his eyes a crack. For a moment he looked at me, but without recognition. Then, with great effort, he turned to his wife and daughter. He whispered a few words that made no sense to me. Screwing up his face, he tried to point at something.

Necla went over to him. 'Do you need something, dear father?'

'Go on, now. Go on outside for a while.' His voice was weak and hoarse.

Mihriye Hanım gestured for me to leave with her and the girl. But when the patient saw her doing this, he reached and grabbed my wrist, and said: 'You stay here!'

His wife and daughter seemed surprised. 'Be careful, dear father! Keep your arms under the covers!'

Raif Efendi nodded hastily, as if to say, 'I know! I know!' Then once again, he gestured for them to leave.

Then he pointed at the package that I was still holding, even though I'd forgotten all about it. 'Did you bring everything?'

At first I just looked at him. I didn't understand what he meant. Was I perhaps wondering why he was making so much of these things? My friend was still staring at me, his eyes bright with anxiety.

Only then did I remember the famous black notebook. I hadn't even bothered to open it up, or wonder about its contents. It had never occurred to me that Raif Efendi might own such a thing.

Tearing open the package, I left the towel and the other bits on a chair behind the door. Picking up the notebook, I took it over to Raif Efendi. 'Is this what you wanted?'

He nodded.

Slowly I leafed through it, as curiosity overtook me. The large and disordered scrawl across its ruled pages spoke of a great haste. I glanced at the first page. There was no title. On the right there was a date: 20 June 1933. Just below it was this line: 'Something strange happened to me yesterday, and it swept me back to that time I thought I'd left behind for ever . . .'

I did not read what followed. Raif Efendi had again taken his arm out from under the blankets to take my hand. 'Don't read it!' he said. Nodding towards the other side of the room, he whispered: 'Throw it in there!'

I turned to look. Behind a sheet of mica I saw the glowing red eyes of a stove.

'You want me to burn it?'

'Yes!'

I was more curious than ever. I could not, would not, let my hands destroy Raif Efendi's notebook.

'What good would that do, Raif Bey?' I said instead. 'Wouldn't it be a shame? What would be the point of destroying a notebook that served as your friend and companion over many long years?'

'It no longer serves any purpose!' he said, and again he nodded towards the stove. 'It's no longer of any use!'

I could see then that there was no talking him out of it. He had, I imagined, poured the soul he'd hidden from us all into these pages, and now he wanted to take it with him.

I looked at this man who wished to leave nothing of himself behind, who, even as he moved towards death, wished to take his loneliness with him. And I wished him everlasting mercy. My own bond with him would last just as long.

'I understand, Raif Bey!' I said. 'I understand only too well. You are right to hold back everything that's yours. You're also right to want to destroy this notebook . . . but can't you wait just one more day?'

With his eyes, he asked me why.

To press my case one last time, I moved closer. I looked into his eyes, hoping that my own would express the love and affection I felt for him.

'Could you not leave this notebook with me for a single night? We've been friends for a long time now, and you've never told me a single thing about yourself . . . Do you really find it strange that I might wish to know more? Do you still feel the need to hide so much from me? To me, you are the most precious person in the world . . . But even so, you want to see me the same way you see everyone else – as a nobody – and abandon me?'

My eyes were filled with tears. My chest was heaving, but still I went on. It was as if all the resentments that had accumulated over many months had to come out all at once: 'You may be right to have no confidence in others. But can't there be exceptions? Can't there? Don't forget, you're human, too . . . You're being selfish, and for nothing!'

There I stopped, thinking this was no way to talk to a man who was gravely ill. He, too, was silent. So I made one last attempt: 'Raif Bey, please try and understand me! I am just embarking on the journey that you are close to finishing. I want to understand people. Most of all I want to understand what people did to you.'

With a violent shake of the head, he cut me short. He was whispering something. I leaned forward, close enough to feel his breath on my face.

'No! No!' he said. 'No one did anything to me . . . not a thing. Not a single thing . . . It was me . . . always me . . . '

Suddenly he stopped. His chin dropped to his chest. He was breathing more rapidly now. Clearly, this scene had exhausted him. For a moment I considered throwing the notebook into the stove and leaving.

Once again, the patient opened his eyes. 'It's nobody's fault! Not even mine!' He could say no more. For now he was coughing. Finally, he indicated the notebook with his eyes. 'Read it! You'll see!'

I slipped the black notebook into my pocket, as fast as if I'd been expecting this all along.

'I'll bring it back tomorrow, and burn it in front of your eyes,' I said. With a carelessness that belied his previous scruples, Raif Efendi shrugged his shoulders, as if to say: 'You can do what you like!'

And I knew then that he was so far gone that he had even severed his connection with this notebook, in which the most important events of his life were recorded. I kissed his hand, to take my leave. When I tried to stand up, he pulled me back, to kiss me first on the forehead and then on the cheeks. When I lifted my head, I saw tears streaming down his face. Unable to hide them or wipe them away, Raif Efendi stared at me unblinking. And I could no longer hold myself back. I, too, was crying – soundlessly, wordlessly, in the face of deep and uncommon sorrow. I had known it would be hard to leave his side. But I'd not known it would bring me such terrible pain.

Once again, Raif Efendi's lips trembled. In a very faint voice, he said: 'In all the time we knew each other, you and I have never spoken for this long . . . What a shame!' With that, he closed his eyes.

And now, it seemed, we had said our farewells. To keep those waiting outside from seeing the state of my face, I rushed through the hall as fast as I could and made for the door. A cold wind dried my eyes as I walked away, muttering, 'What a shame! What a shame!'

Back at the hotel, I found my roommate asleep. Slipping into bed, I turned on the lamp on my bedside table, and began at once to read what Raif Efendi had recorded between the black covers of his notebook.

20 June 1933

Something strange happened to me yesterday, and it sent me reeling back to that time I thought I'd left behind for ever. Now I know these memories will never leave me . . . One chance encounter, and I am cruelly awake, wrenched from the numb lethargy that has kept me going these last ten years. I would be lying if I said this could drive me mad, or be the death of me. People somehow manage to accustom themselves to what they first think insufferable. I, too, shall endure . . . But how? I look into the future, and all I see is a life of cruel torment. Somehow, I shall find a way to bear it . . . just as I have done until now . . .

But I cannot go on with all this locked up inside me. There are things – so many things – that I need to say . . . but to whom? . . . Can there be another soul wandering this great globe who is as lonely as I? Who would hear me out? Where would I begin? I cannot recall saying anything to anyone over the past ten years. I have needlessly fled from society, need-lessly driven people away. But what else can I do now? There's no going back. It would serve no purpose. This can only mean that it was meant to be. If only I could find the words . . . If only I had someone to confide in . . . But how would I find him? I wouldn't know where to look. And even if did, I still wouldn't. Why, after all, did I buy this notebook? If I had a fleck of hope, would I be sitting here now, going against the habits of a lifetime and writing these words? But sometimes people need to unburden themselves . . . If only yesterday hadn't happened . . . Oh, if only I had not stumbled upon the truth . . . I might have gone on living as before, with my small comforts . . .

I was walking down the street yesterday when I chanced upon two people. One of them I was meeting for the first time, the other was perhaps more distant from me than anyone else on this earth. Who could have imagined that these two would have the power to undo me?

Enough! If I am to tell this story, I must do so calmly, starting from the beginning . . . I must, in effect, go back a good few years: ten, to be precise, or twelve . . . perhaps even fifteen . . . but visiting them afresh. Perhaps, by wandering through those years, by occupying them fully, the terrors and the trivial details, I can set myself free. Perhaps what I will write will not be nearly as painful as what I have lived and it will bring me some relief. When I come to see how some of it was neither as simple nor complicated as I had thought, I might even find my ardour somewhat shaming . . . perhaps . . .

My father was from Havran. I, too, was born and raised there. I received my early education in the same place, moving on to a high school an hour away, in Edremit. Towards the close of the Great War, at the age of eighteen, I was drafted into the army, but the armistice was declared before I saw active duty. Returning home, I went back to high school but failed to graduate. I'd never been very keen on my studies. The chaos of my year away had drained me of all interest.

Following the armistice, all semblance of order disappeared. There was no working government, nor was there any sense of shared ideas or aims. Several territories had fallen to foreign troops and suddenly a host of gangs of varying notoriety came to life, some opening up new fronts against the enemy and others plundering local villages; a bandit celebrated one day as a hero was driven away a week later, whereupon it was announced that his body was hanging in the village square of Konakönü, near Edremit. At a time like this, it made no sense to hide away indoors and read Ottoman history or treatises on ethics. However, my father, who was thought to be one of the wealthier men in those parts, remained adamant that I should have an education. Seeing so many of my peers strap on ammunition belts and throw rifles over their shoulders to join rebel units, only to be killed by bandits or enemy forces, he began to fear for my future. The truth is that I did not want to remain idle and was already making my own plans in secret. But then enemy forces took command of our village and all my heroic fantasies came to naught.

For a few months I drifted. Most of my friends had disappeared. My father decided to send me to Istanbul. He didn't know any more than I did where I might go. 'Find a school and study there,' he said. Which goes to show how little he knew his son. Though I had always been an awkward and reclusive boy, I did have a secret yearning. There had been one lesson in which I had won my teacher's admiration: I could paint fairly well. I had dreamed, from time to time, of attending Istanbul's Academy of Fine Arts. That said, I had always been one of those quiet boys who preferred dreams to the real world. I was, in addition, absurdly shy, and therefore often mistaken for a fool, which upset me deeply. For nothing terrified me more than the prospect of correcting a false impression. Though I was often blamed for mistakes made by my classmates, I never dared to say a word in self-defence. I would simply go home to hide in a corner and cry. I can well remember how my mother and – even more – my father would throw up their hands and say: 'Honestly, you should have been born a girl!' My greatest pleasure was to sit alone beside the river, or in the far corner of the garden, and let my thoughts waft away. My daydreams were in sharp contrast to real life; they were full of adventures and heroic deeds. Like the heroes in the countless novels I had read in translation, I was possessed of a sweet and mysterious desire; in my case a girl named Fahriye who lived in the neighbourhood next to ours. Gathering around me the loyal comrades with whom I wreaked havoc over distant lands, I would don my mask, strap my two guns to my waist, and sally forth, to sweep her off to a magnificent cave in the mountains. I would imagine how first she would be shaking with fear, but once she saw how my own men trembled in my presence, once she had taken stock of the cave's unrivalled riches, awe would overcome her, and when at last she looked me in the eye, it would be to throw her arms around me, crying with untrammelled delight. Sometimes I would travel through Africa like a famous explorer, living among the cannibals, seeing lands no eye had ever seen; at other times I was a famous painter touring Europe. Though it was the authors I read – Michel Zevaco, Jules Verne, Alexandre Dumas, Ahmet Mithat Efendi and Vecihi Bey – who painted my imagination.

Father hated my reading all the time, and sometimes he threw away my books. Some nights he refused to let me turn on the light in my bedroom. But I could always find a way, and after he caught me reading *Les Misérables* or *The Mysteries of Paris* by the light of a little string-wick lamp, he gave up and left me to it. I read everything I could get my hands on and whatever I read – be it the adventures of Monsieur LeCoq or the history of Murat Bey – it left its mark on me.

There was, for instance, a history of the Roman Empire, in which an ambassador by the name of Mucius Scaevola, while negotiating a treaty, was told that he was to accept the terms offered, on pain of death: his response was to plunge his arm into a fire and continue with his deliberations, in absolute calm. Inspired by his unflinching courage, I proceeded to test my own powers of resilience by plunging my own hand into the fire, only to burn my fingers badly. I can still see that ambassador, smiling calmly through his pain. There was a time when I tried my hand at writing; indeed, I even scribbled a few little poems, but I quickly abandoned my efforts. No matter what I had bottled up inside me, I was absurdly anxious about letting it out, and so my adventures in writing ended. I did, however, carry on painting. There was, I thought, no risk of revealing anything personal. If I took something from the outside world and brought it to life on paper, I was a catalyst and nothing more. With time, however, I came to understand that this was not the case, and so I gave up painting too ... Always that fear ...

In Istanbul, at the Academy of Fine Arts, I quickly – and without assistance – came to the conclusion that painting was a mode of expression, and, inevitably, of self-expression, and after that there seemed no point in continuing my studies. In any case my teachers didn't see much in me. I only ever presented my most trivial efforts: if my works expressed anything personal, or exposed any personal particularity, I went to extreme lengths to hide them away, lest they ever see the light of day. If someone ever happened to find one, I would gasp like a naked woman caught in an intimate moment, and rush away blushing.

Unsure of what to do next, I spent some time wandering the streets of Istanbul. Those were the years of the armistice and the city was so unseemly and chaotic that I could hardly bear it. I asked my father for money so that I might return to Havran. Ten days later I received a long letter. It was his last effort to get me to make something of myself.

Somewhere he had heard that the currency in Germany had tumbled and that foreigners in particular could live there quite comfortably: one could get by on much less than in Istanbul. Instructing me to go there to learn about the soap business, scented soaps in particular, he went on to announce that he was sending me the money needed to cover my expenses. I was overjoyed. Not because I was interested in the art of soap-making – rather, I was delighted because, at the moment I least expected it, I was being offered a chance to visit Europe – since childhood the home of my fondest dreams. 'Spend a couple of years learning the trade,' my father had written, 'then you can come home and work on improving our soap factories. I shall make you a manager. Once you have established your-self in the world of business, you are sure to find happiness and prosperity.' Yet that was last thing on my mind . . .

My plan was to learn a foreign language and read books in that language and, most importantly, discover Europe – meet face to face the people I had so far encountered only in books. For weren't they the ones who had nurtured my wayward nature and lured me so far from home?

I was ready within a week. I travelled to Germany on a train that took me through Bulgaria. I only spoke Turkish. Drawing on three or four phrases I had memorized from a pocket language guide I studied during the four-day journey, I was able to make my way to the *pension* whose address I had jotted down in my notebook while still in Istanbul.

I spent the first few weeks learning enough German to sur-vive and wandering the streets in a state of wonder. But that didn't last long. In the end, this was just another city. The streets were a bit wider, and much cleaner, and the inhabitants were blonder. However, there was nothing here to sweep me off my feet. Knowing so little about the Europe of my imagina-tion, I had no way to measure it against the city in which I now lived . . . I had yet to learn that nothing in this world can ever match the marvels that we conjure up in our own minds.

Assuming that I would not be able to begin work until I had learned the language, I started taking lessons from a retired officer who had learned a little Turkish during the war. The manageress of the *pension* was eager to spend her free time prattling to me and this was much to my benefit. The *pension's* other guests, meanwhile, found it amusing to befriend a Turk and they bombarded me with all manner of silly questions. There was a lively crowd around the dinner table. Three in particular took me under their wing: a Dutch widow named Frau van Tiedemann, a Portuguese trader named Herr Camera, who imported oranges from the Canary Islands, and the elderly Herr Döppke. He had been doing business in the colony of Cameroon; leaving everything behind after the armistice, he had returned to his homeland. Here he led a humble existence, devoting his days to the political meetings that were all the rage then, and in the evening he would return to the *pension* to share his impressions. On a number of occasions, he would bring back newly discharged and still unemployed German officers with whom he would speak for hours. From what I could piece together, they were of the view that Germany would only be saved if another man with Bismarck's iron will came to power to rebuild the army and avenge the injustices of the past with another world war.

From time to time a resident would leave, to be replaced by someone new. But over time I grew accustomed to these changes of cast. I came to tire of the red lamps that lit the dark room where we took our meals, and the constant smell of cabbage, and the heated political discussions that accompanied every meal. The discussions in particular . . . Everyone had an idea as to how to save Germany. However, none of these proposals had anything to do with Germany. Rather, they were tied to personal interests. An old woman who had lost her fortune through money-mongering was angry with the officers, who were angry with the striking workers. She blamed the soldiers for Germany's defeat, while the colonial tradesman for no apparent reason was forever blasting the emperor's declaration of war. Even the housekeeper started discussing politics with me when she came to tidy up my room in the morning, and whenever she had a moment free she buried herself in the newspaper. She, too, had florid opinions, and whenever she expressed them, she would shake her fists and turn beet-red.

It was as if I had forgotten why I had come to Germany. Whenever I received a letter from Father I was reminded of the soap trade and I would write back saying that I was still learning German: very soon, I assured him, I would seek a suitable training college. By saying this, I was deluding both him and myself. The days slipped by, each one much the same as the other. I explored every part of the city. I visited the museums and the zoo. In the space of a few months I had, I thought, seen all that this city of millions had to offer, and this plunged me into despair. 'So this is Europe,' I said to myself. 'Why all the fuss?' From here it was a short road to the conclusion that the world itself was a place of little interest. Most afternoons I spent wandering through the crowds along the broad avenues, watching men heading home, their grave expressions speaking of important business, or women with vapid smiles and languorous eyes, hanging onto the arms of men who still marched like soldiers.

So as not to tell my father an outright lie, I managed, with the help of several Turkish friends, to present myself to a manufacturer of luxury soap. The German employees of this firm, which was owned by a larger concern in Sweden, gave me a warm reception – they had not forgotten that we had been brothers in battle – but they were reluctant to explain their processes in any detail, as least compared to what I had learned in

Havran, and I suppose that was because they were safeguarding company secrets.

Or perhaps they were like that because they saw no real ambition in me and did not wish to waste their time. Eventually I stopped going to the factory altogether. They never got back in touch. My father was by now writing less frequently, while I carried on living in Berlin without ever wondering what I was going to do next, or why I had come here in the first place.

I was still taking German lessons from the army officer three evenings a week. I spent my days visiting museums and newly opened galleries. Returning to the *pension* in the evening, I'd catch my first whiff of cabbage from a distance of a hundred paces. But I was no longer as bored as I'd been in the early months. For now I was slowly learning to read properly in German and this gave me great pleasure. Before long, it was akin to an addiction. Lying face down on the bed, I would open my book and stay there for hours, a thick, old dictionary at my side. In many cases I would not even bother to riffle through it, as I was able to glean the meaning of a word from its context. A new world had opened itself up to me. I had moved beyond the translated literature of my childhood, in which heroic figures embarked on unrivalled adventures. The books I was now reading spoke of people like me, of the world I saw and heard around me. They spoke of things I had witnessed but not really grasped. Now their true meanings began to emerge. I was influenced most profoundly by the Russians. I read all of the great Turgenev's stories in one sitting. One in particular left my mind spinning for many days. The heroine in the story, the young Klara Milich, falls in love with a naive young man, but she is unable to divulge her true feelings. Instead, she decides to punish herself for falling in love with a fool, and hands herself over to addiction. I don't know why, but I felt a particularly close bond with this young woman. When I saw how she was incapable of voicing her true feelings, and how fear and envy contrived to suppress everything about her that was deep and strong, and beautiful – I saw myself.

By then my life had been much enriched by the paintings of the old masters in Berlin's museums. There were times when, after gazing at a painting in the National Gallery for many hours, I could conjure up that face, or that landscape, for many days.

I had been in Germany for almost a year by now. One dark and rainy day in November – how clearly I remember it – I was skimming the newspaper when I noticed an article about an exhibition of new painters. In truth, I did not know what to make of this new generation. Perhaps I didn't like them because their work was too bold, and going to any lengths to catch the eye. I found that mode of self-promotion alien and distasteful. And so I passed over this article without bothering to read it. But a few hours later I was out on my daily stroll through the city when I happened to find myself standing in front of the building where that exhibition was being held. I had no pressing business. So I took a chance and stepped inside. Slowly I wandered through the exhibition, surveying the paintings, large and small, with no little indifference.

Most of them made me want to laugh: there were people with cubic shoulders and knees and heads and breasts of disproportionate sizes, and landscapes portrayed in stark colours, made of something like crepe paper. Crystal vases as shapeless as the shards of broken bricks, flowers as lifeless as if they had been pressed inside books for many years, and finally these dreadful portraits that looked like the sketches of criminals . . . Yet the visitors were enjoying themselves. Perhaps I should have dismissed these artists for presuming they could achieve great height from such little effort. But when I considered the twisted pleasure they might gain from being punished and ridiculed, I could only pity them.

Suddenly, near the door to the main room, I stopped. Even now, after all these years, I cannot describe the torrent that swept through me in that moment. I only remember standing, transfixed, before a portrait of a woman wearing a fur coat. Others pushed past me, impatient to see the rest of the exhibition, but I could not move. What was it about that portrait? I know that words alone will not suffice. All I can say is that she wore a strange, formidable, haughty and almost wild expression, one that I had never seen before on a woman. But while that face was utterly new to me, I couldn't help but feel that I had seen her many times before. Surely I knew this pale face, this dark brown hair, this dark brow, these dark eyes that spoke of eternal anguish and resolve. I had known that woman since I'd opened my first book at the age of seven – since I'd started, at the age of five, to dream. I saw in her echoes of Halit Ziya Uşaklıgil's Nihal, Vecihi Bey's Mehcure, and Cavalier Buridan's beloved. I saw the Cleopatra I had come to know in history books, and Muhammad's mother, Amine Hatun, of whom I had dreamed while listening to the Mevlit prayers. She was a swirling blend of all the women I had ever imagined. Dressed in the pelt of a wildcat, she was mostly in shadow, but for a sliver of a pale white neck, and an oval face was turned slightly to the left. Her dark eyes were lost in thought, absently staring into the distance, drawing on a last wisp of hope as she searched for something that she was almost certain she would never find. Yet mixed in with the sadness was a sort of challenge. It was as if she were saying, 'Yes, I know. I won't find what I'm looking for . . . and what of it?' The same challenge was playing on her plump lips. The lower lip was slightly fuller. Her eyelids were somewhat swollen. Her eyebrows were neither thick nor thin but short. The dark-brown hair that framed her broad forehead fell down over her cheeks, and her fur coat. Her pointed chin was slightly upturned. Her nose was long, her nostrils flared.

My hands were almost trembling as I flipped through the exhibition catalogue. I was hoping I might find out more about the painting. At the bottom of a page at the very end, I found just three words beside the number of the painting: Maria Puder, *Selbstporträt*. Nothing else. Clearly the artist had no other work in the exhibition. I was not unhappy about that. I was afraid her other paintings might not have the same overwhelming effect on me and indeed diminish my initial admiration. I stayed until late. Occasionally I got up and wandered through the gallery, looking blindly at the other paintings, but soon I came back to the same place to gaze at that one painting. Each time it seemed as if I could see new expressions in her face, as if she were slowly coming to life. Her downcast eyes seemed to be glancing at me and her lips, I thought, were fluttering.

With time, the gallery emptied out. The tall man at the door must, I thought, be waiting for me to leave. Quickly I stood up and left. A soft rain was falling over the city. For once, I made straight for the *pension* without dawdling along the way. I was desperate to get through dinner and retire to my room, to conjure up the image of that face. I didn't say a word over dinner.

'Where did you go today?' asked Frau Heppner, the manageress.

'Nowhere in particular,' I replied. 'I took a stroll and then visited a gallery with an exhibition of modern art.'

Everyone else at the table launched into a discussion about modern art, and I slipped out of the room.

As I was taking off my jacket, my newspaper fell out of the pocket. I leaned over and picked it up and as I was placing it on my desk, my heart skipped a beat. This was the paper with the article about the exhibition I had read that morning in a café. I tore it open to see if there was anything in the article about the painting or the artist. It surprised me to be behaving so rashly because I was in fact a gentle, unemotional man. I scanned the article from the beginning, and suddenly stopped at the name I had seen in the catalogue: Maria Puder.

Considering that she was a young artist exhibiting her work for the first time, the article gave her a fair amount of attention. It claimed she was interested in following in the footsteps of the great masters, showing a fine and admirable talent for capturing an expression. In sharp contrast to most other self-portraits, she did not fall prey to a 'stubborn ugliness', nor did she go in pursuit of an 'exaggerated beauty'. After touching on a few technical matters, the critic concluded by saying that (by uncanny coincidence) the woman in the painting bore, in both expression and manner, a striking resemblance to Andrea del Sarto's depiction of the Mother Mary in his *Madonna delle Arpie*. In a slightly humorous tone, he wished the 'Madonna in a Fur Coat' every success, before moving on to discuss another work that had caught his eye.

Early the next morning, I went to a shop renowned for its reproductions and searched for the Madonna of the Harpies. I found her in a large album featuring Del Sarto's work. Although it was a poor reproduction that failed to give much sense of the original, I could see that the critic was right. Standing on a pedestal and with the holy child in her arms, the Madonna was gazing at the ground, heedless of both the bearded man to her right and the young man on her left; in the tilt of her head and in her face and on her lips, I could clearly see the same expression of anguish and resentment that I had caught in the painting the day before. As the pages from these albums were sold separately, I was able to buy the reproduction and take it back to my room. After studying the work carefully, I was convinced that it was a work of great value. For the first time in my life I was truly looking at the Madonna. In all the other depictions of Mother Mary that I had seen until now, she wore an expression of such innocence as to render the work absurd; in those paintings she resembled either a little girl looking down at a baby in her arms as if to say, 'Have you seen? Have you seen the gift God has given me?', or a chambermaid staring blankly at a child who has come crashing into her world, courtesy of a man they cannot name.

But the Mother Mary in Sarto's painting had learned how to think, she had developed her own ideas on how to live, she was a woman, no less, who had begun to shun the world. She paid no heed to the supplicating saints beside her, or the Messiah in her arms. She was not even looking up at the sky; instead, she had her eyes on the ground, and no doubt she saw something there.

I left the picture on my desk. I closed my eyes and imagined the painting in the exhibition. Only then did it occur to me that the woman depicted in the painting must exist in real life. Yes, of course. It was a self-portrait! Which meant that this miracle of a woman was living among us, her deep dark eyes gazing at the ground or at the person across the way, her lips parted to speak, her lower lip slightly larger than the other . . . she existed! She was alive! Somewhere, sometime, I might even catch sight of her . . . When the possibility first struck me, it was as an overwhelming fear. For a man of no experience like me, it was nothing short of terrifying to think of coming face to face with a woman such as her.

Although I was twenty-four years old by then, I had never had an adventure with a woman. In Havran there had been various drunken exploits and the odd flight of debauchery led by the older neighbourhood boys, which I never managed to make any sense of. My natural reticence stopped me from ever mustering enough courage to try again. The only women I knew were the creatures that stirred my imagination. They might feature in the thousand and one fantasies I concocted as I lay under olive trees on hot summer nights, far from material concerns, but they all had one thing in common: they were beyond my reach. I had, of course, been secretly in love with our neighbour Fahriye for many years. In my dreams, I had explored improprieties that bordered on the shameful. Whenever I passed her on the street, my face would turn so red and my heart beat so fast, that I'd soon be ducking for cover. On Ramadan nights, I would steal away from the house and find myself a hiding place near their front door, to watch her come out with her mother, who'd be holding a lantern. But once the door was open, I could barely make them out in their long, dark coats, cocooned in that soft yellow light. Turning away, I would tremble for fear that they might see me, as they left for the Tarawih prayers.

If ever I met a woman I found attractive, my first thought was to run away. From the moment we came face to face, I lived in dread that my every glance and movement might reveal my true feelings. Drowning in shame, I became the most miserable person on earth. I cannot recall ever looking directly at a woman during my adolescence, not even my mother. Later, when I moved to Istanbul, I made an effort to overcome my absurd shyness; through friends, I met a few girls with whom I could be myself. But the moment I sensed a spark of interest on their part, all my courage drained away. I was never innocent: when I entertained these women in my mind, I would engineer scenes that even the most masterful lover would have found daunting, and when I imagined these girls' smouldering lips pressed against mine, it seemed to me an intoxication far greater than anything real life could bring.

But this painting of the Madonna in a Fur Coat had shaken me – so much so that the very thought of imagining her in such a scene was impossible. I could not begin to imagine it. I could not even imagine sitting beside her as a friend. All I wanted was to stand before that painting for hours on end, gazing into those dark, unseeing eyes. And the desire to do so only grew. I threw on my coat and headed back to the gallery. It went on like that for days.

Every afternoon, I would stroll in, pretending to stop to inspect each painting in the gallery, as my impatience grew. For all I wanted was to go straight to my Madonna. When at last I reached it, I would make as if I had noticed the painting for the first time. And there I would remain, until the doors of the gallery were about to close. I soon became a familiar figure to the guards and the handful of artists who visited the gallery as often as I did. They would greet me with wide smiles, and follow this strange art enthusiast with their eyes. In the end I gave up masking my intentions. I would walk straight to the Madonna in a Fur Coat, settling myself down on the bench across from it. I would stare and stare, until I could stare no longer, and had to cast my eyes down to the floor.

Inevitably, people noticed and were curious. And then one day my worst fear came true. Most of the artists who frequented the gallery were men with large foulards and long hair that tumbled down over their dark suits, but there was also a young woman who joined them from time to time. I thought she must be a painter too.

One day she came over to me. 'It seems you are particularly fascinated by this painting,' she said. 'You come to look at it every day.'

I looked up, to be undone by a knowing, mocking smile. To save myself, I looked down. But there, just ahead of me, were her pointed shoes, waiting for me to explain myself. As my eyes travelled upwards, I noticed that her skirt was short and her legs uncommonly shapely. And I could, every time she moved, almost see a sweet wave rippling down her stockings, all the way to her knees.

Seeing that she was not going to leave until she got an answer from me, I said: 'Yes! It's a beautiful painting . . .' Then, for some reason, I felt the need to offer an explanation. I mumbled a lie: 'She looks a lot like my mother . . .'

'Ah, so that's why you come and look at it for so long!'

'Yes!'

'Is your mother dead?'

'No!'

She waited as if she wanted me to go on. Still staring at the floor, I added: 'She's far away.'

'Oh . . . where is that?'

'In Turkey.'

'Are you Turkish?'

'Yes.'

'I knew you were a foreigner.'

Letting out a little laugh, she sat down next to me on the bench. Her manner could only be described as brazen. Throwing one leg over the other, she revealed her leg well above the knee. I realized then that I was blushing – yet again. Greatly amused by my discomfort, she asked me another question:

'Don't you have a picture of your mother?'

Such impertinence! I thought. She had, I realized, come here only to mock me. The other painters were watching us from a distance and – I was sure of it – smirking.

'I do but . . . this is something else,' I said.

'Oh! So *this* is something else.'

With this, she let out another little laugh.

I made as if to leave. Taking note of this, she said: 'Don't let me disturb you. I was just going . . . Let me leave you alone with your mother.'

Standing up, she began to walk away. Then suddenly she wheeled around and came back over to me. Her voice now bore no resemblance to the one I'd just heard: it was solemn, even mournful: 'Would you truly like to have a mother like that?'

'Yes . . . oh yes, I would.'

'Oh . . .'

Turning her back on me yet again, she sauntered away. I raised my eyes and watched. Her short hair bounced against the back of her neck; with her hands in her pockets, her coat was snug around her hips.

Thinking how those last words of mine had exposed the lie in our first exchange, I did not dare look around me, as I jumped to my feet and fled.

And I left feeling as empty as if I had parted too quickly from a travelling companion I had come to rely on. I knew that I would never set foot in the gallery again. People – people who understood nothing of one another – had driven me away.

Returning to the *pension*, I contemplated the dull days that lay ahead. Every time I sat at the supper table, it would be to listen to middle-class people berating the inflation that was eroding their fortunes, or dictating how Germany was to be saved. Every night, I would go back up to my room, to read stories by Turgenev or Theodor Storm. I saw then that over the past fortnight, my life had begun to take on meaning. I saw, too, what it would mean to lose it. A shaft of light had passed over me, illuminating my empty life with possibilities I dared not question. But now, just as mysteriously, it had vanished. Only now did I understand what this meant. For as long as I could remember, I had – perhaps without knowing, or perhaps not daring to breathe the thought – been searching for someone. That was why I had been avoiding all others. If only for a moment, the painting had convinced me that I might find her, and find her soon. It had sparked in me a hope that would never sink into despair. Shunning the society of others, I withdrew into myself. I cursed the world around me, with greater vehemence than ever before. I considered writing to my father, to tell him I was ready to come home. But what would I say when he asked me what I had learned in Europe? Better, I thought, to remain a few more months and master the perfumed soap trade, just to please him. I went back to the Swedish company and although they did not greet me with the same warmth as before, they agreed to take me on. And each day I reported to the factory for work. I took diligent notes, recording their methods and formulae. I read the books.

Back at the *pension*, the Dutch widow Frau van Tiedemann was paying me a great deal of attention. She would lend me the novels she'd bought for her ten-year-old son at boarding school, and ask for my thoughts. Sometimes, after supper, she would come to my room on some petty pretext and chatter away for hours. Mostly she wanted to know about any adventures I might be having with German girls, and when I told her the truth she'd narrow her eyes, wag her finger and give me a knowing smile, as if to say, 'You can't fool me – I know what young men like you get up to!' One day she invited me out for an afternoon stroll and on our way back she talked me into stopping at a beer hall, where we drank enough to lose track of the time. I'd had the occasional beer since I'd come to Berlin, but never as much as that night. After my head began to spin, I found myself in Frau van Tiedemann's arms. When I came to my senses some moments later, the good-hearted woman was wiping my face with a napkin she'd had the waiters moisten for her. I said that we needed to get home at once. She insisted on paying the bill. When we stepped outside, I noticed that she was staggering as much as I was. Arm in arm, we stumbled forward, swaying into the path of those coming the other way. It was late by now, so the streets weren't too crowded. Then, as we were crossing a street, something strange happened. Stepping up onto the pavement, Frau van Tiedemann caught her foot on the kerb; plump as she was, the woman grabbed onto me to steady herself, and I suppose it was because she was taller than me that she ended up with her arms around my neck. But after she had regained her balance, she didn't let go; instead, she gripped me more tightly. And perhaps it was because I was drunk, but I had lost all inhibitions. Wrapping my arms around her, I felt the hungry lips of a thirty-five-year-old woman exploring mine. I breathed in her warm breath and with it the pungent, intoxicating perfume of passion. A number of passers-by laughed and wished us happiness. Then, about ten paces ahead, I caught sight of a woman walking towards us, under a street lamp. A shock passed through me. Whereupon Frau van Tiedemann tightened her embrace, passing her lips over my hair. But by now I was struggling to free myself. All I wanted was to see the woman walking towards us. It was she. A single glance and lightning flashed, clearing the fog in my mind. For here she was: the pale, long-nosed, dark-eyed woman draped in the skin of a wildcat, my Madonna in a Fur Coat. How sad she looked, and how weary, as she walked down the street, oblivious to the world around her! But when she saw us, she stopped in surprise. Our eyes met. In hers I saw the flicker of a smile. I winced, as if lashed by a whip. Although I was drunk, I felt it would have been distasteful to have met her under such circumstances. Her smile made her verdict clear. At last I freed myself from the old woman's grip. I dashed off after the Madonna in a Fur Coat, hoping I might catch her. Not knowing what I would say or do, I went as far as the corner. She was gone. I stood there for a few minutes, searching all around me, but there was no one. No one but Frau van Tiedemann: 'What's come over you? Out with it, what's happened?' Linking arms, she led me back to the *pension*. All the way, she kept a tight hold of me, pressing her face against mine. But now her warm breath seemed intolerable, oppressive . . . All the same I didn't resist. I had, after all, never learned how. The best I had ever managed was to run away and now that seemed to be out of the question. I couldn't take three steps without the woman pulling me back into her arms. And at the same time I was still reeling from my surprise encounter. As the effects of the alcohol wore off, I tried to recall what I had just seen. But those smiling eyes were lost again. It was as if I had dreamt them. No, I thought, I must not have seen her. I could never have met her under such circumstances. What I'd seen was a nightmare, born of that woman who had taken me into her arms, to smother me with her kisses and hot breath . . . I longed for nothing more than to escape to my bed, to let go of my cheap fantasies and let sleep do its work. But the woman had no intention of letting me go. The closer we came to the *pension*, the tighter and more passionate her grip.

On the stairs she wrapped her arms around my neck again. Somehow managing to wrest myself free, I dashed up to the next landing. Her massive body made the staircase tremble as she hurried after me, panting heavily. As I fumbled with my key, Herr Döppke, the colonialist, appeared at the other end of the corridor. Slowly he approached me. I realized then that he had stayed up waiting for our return, and I took a deep breath. Everyone in the *pension* knew that this gentleman (who was quite well off) had fond feelings for the widow in whom the flames of passion still stirred. Indeed, Frau van Tiedemann was not entirely unaware of his affections, and it was rumoured that she herself had fond designs on the mighty old bachelor, whose spritely demeanour belied his fifty years. Catching sight of each other, the two friends stopped short. At once I slipped into my room, locking the door behind me. A hushed conversation ensued. It went on for some time. Careful questions were met with careful answers, soothing the ears of those anxious to believe. At long last I heard footsteps, as whispers followed them down the corridor.

The moment my head hit the pillow, I fell asleep. Towards dawn I had a nightmare in which the Madonna in a Fur Coat appeared in many guises, each time crushing me with her magnificent smile. I kept trying to say something, to explain something, but I couldn't. The glint in her dark eyes rendered me mute. She had delivered her verdict, and there was nothing left for me to do but writhe in despair. I woke up before sunrise. My head ached. I switched on the lamp and tried reading. But the lines kept furring up, and from the mist beyond I could see two dark eyes laughing at my sorry state. As sure as I was that what I had seen the night before had been only in my mind, I was unable to calm myself. I got dressed and went out. It was a cold and damp Berlin morning. There was no one else on the street but delivery boys pushing handcarts loaded down with milk and butter and little loaves of bread. Rounding the corner, I saw policemen tearing down revolutionary posters that had been plastered to the wall in the night. Following the canal, I walked as far as the Tiergarten. Two swans were gliding through the still waters, as motionless as toys. The meadows and the benches in the woods were wet. On one of them there was a crumpled newspaper and several hairpins. They reminded me of the previous night. Frau van Tiedemann must have dropped quite a few hairpins on her way back from the beer hall, I imagined, and now, most likely, she was lying happily beside her neighbour Herr Döppke, thinking about how she would need to rise early enough to return to her room before the maids arrived.

Arriving at the factory earlier than ever, I greeted the guard warmly. From now on I would throw myself into my work, thereby freeing myself of the oppressive fears to which my idle life had condemned me. I sat down beside the great soap vats. Breathing in the essence of rose, I made endless notes in my journal. As I wrote down the names of the factories that made soap presses, I was already imagining myself as the manager of a large, modern soap factory in Havran, famed throughout Turkey. I imagined pink, egg-shaped soaps labelled Mehmet Raif – Havran, wrapped in soft, scented paper.

By afternoon my spirits had lifted, for I could at last begin to imagine a brighter future. For too long I had been fretting over nothing, giving myself over to flights of fancy and succumbing to invented fears. But now I was going to change. I was going to confine my reading to books that would help me in my career. Why should someone like me, born of an affluent family, not find happiness?

I had my father's olive groves, two factories and a soapworks waiting for me in Havran. My two older sisters, both married to wealthy men, would each have a share in the business and I would lead the life of a respected businessman. The Turkish army had driven out enemy forces and freed Havran. In his letters, my father was elated and overflowing with patriotic sentiment. Even in Berlin, we enjoyed a victory celebration at the Turkish embassy. Occasionally I would come out of my shell and offer advice to Herr Döppke and the unemployed officers on the best way to rescue Germany, in the light of our achievements in Anatolia. There was, I told myself, everything to live for. Why fret about a meaningless painting, a figment inspired by characters in books? No, from now on I was going to change . . .

But by nightfall, my spirits had dipped again. Not wishing to face Frau van Tiedemann at supper, I decided to eat out, and drank two tankards of beer. But no matter how hard I tried, I could not pull myself back up. It felt as if something were pressing down on my heart. Thinking that a walk in the fresh air might help me to banish my foul mood, I called for the bill. The sky was overcast and it was spitting rain. In the low clouds I could see the crimson reflection of the city's lights. I had arrived at a long, wide avenue called Kurfürstendamm. Here the entire sky was illuminated, casting an orange light on the rain as it fell. The street was lined with casinos, theatres and cinemas. Crowds were strolling up and down, oblivious to the rain. I joined the procession, as my mind ran in circles. It was almost as if I were trying to free myself of a thought that had taken me captive. I read every sign I passed, and every illuminated advertisement. Over and over, I walked the full length of the avenue, which extends for several kilometres. Then I turned right and made for Wittenberg Square.

Here I found a group of young men dressed in red boots whose faces were painted like women. They were loitering on the pavement outside a large store named KaDeWe, flashing flirtatious looks at the people passing by. I pulled out my watch. It was after eleven o'clock. It was that late already. I quickened my steps as I walked the short distance to Nollendorf Square. Now I knew where I was going. I was going to the spot where, the night before, at precisely this time, I had met the Madonna in a Fur Coat. The square was deserted, except for a few policemen outside the theatre on the northern side. Crossing the street, I arrived at the spot where I had stumbled about with Frau van Tiedemann. I kept my eyes fixed on the lamp post, as if this alone might conjure up the woman I so longed to see. Despite having convinced myself that what I'd seen the night before was a chimera, a fantasy born of a drunken stupor, I was here now, waiting for a woman who might be no more than a hallucination. In place of those factories I'd been dreaming up since morning, there was only a breeze. Once again, I had revealed myself to be a puppet of my imagination, a captive of the make-believe.

Then I saw someone passing through the square and coming towards me. Hiding in the doorway of a house, I waited. Peering out, I saw the Madonna coming towards me, her steps clipped and sharp. This time there was no mistake. I was sober. The empty street echoed the dry click of her boots. I felt my aching heart contracting as it pounded against my chest. The footsteps were coming closer now. Turning my back to the street, I pretended to be fiddling with the door, leaning over as if I were about to push it open and slip inside. It was all I could do not to fall or yelp when I heard the footsteps stop right behind me. I held onto the wall. Once she had passed by, I came out of the doorway and followed her, keeping close for fear of losing her. I couldn't see her face. But here I was – the man who had felt such terror at the prospect of ever seeing her again – just five or six steps behind her. She didn't seem to have noticed me. But then, why had I come here and waited for her, if I was just going to hide? Why had I come back to this place at all? And why was I now following her? Was it really her? How could I be so certain that a woman passing down a particular street at some random hour of the night would pass through the very spot again exactly twenty-four hours later? I was in no state to answer any of these questions. My heart still pounding, I continued to follow her, though with every step I grew more fearful that she might suddenly swing around and see me. I kept my head bowed, eyes fixed on the tarmac, following the sound of her footsteps. Suddenly the clacking disappeared. I stopped in my tracks. My head hanging even lower, I must have looked like a prisoner. But no one came over to me, no one asked: 'Why are you following me?' A few seconds later I noticed that the street around my feet was brightly lit.

Slowly I raised my head: there wasn't a woman in sight. A few steps ahead of me, I saw the shimmering door of the Atlantic, a well-known cabaret. Its name, blazoned in blinking blue lights across a gigantic sign, sailed upon a sea of electric blue waves. At the door was a man nearly two metres tall, wearing a sequined suit and a red hat. He invited me inside. The woman must already have gone in, I thought. Without a moment's hesitation, I leaned close to the man and said: 'Did a woman in a fur coat walking ahead of me go inside?'

The doorman leaned even closer. 'Yes,' he said. He smiled knowingly.

Could this woman be a regular? I wondered. If she came here every night at the same time, she might well be. Breathing in deeply, but also calmly, I took off my coat and stepped inside.

The hall was packed. In the centre was a circular dance floor, and behind it an orchestra. Along the walls were rows of tall, discreet, private boxes. Their curtains were mostly drawn; from time to time couples would emerge to dance for a time before returning to their box, again to draw the curtains. Crossing over to a table that looked to be empty, I sat down and ordered a beer. My heart was no longer racing. Calmly, I took in the scene. I was hoping that I would find her – the Madonna in a Fur Coat, the woman who had left me sleepless for weeks – sitting at one of these tables, beside a Casanova young or old. Once I had had the time to get the measure of this woman to whom I had attached such significance – once I saw her offering herself up on the market – I would be free of her. I could not see her at any of the tables around the dance floor. Most likely she was in one of the private boxes. I smiled bitterly. I scolded myself for failing to see people as they truly were. Although I was twenty-four years old, I had not yet freed myself of the naivety of youth. I had allowed myself to be possessed by a simple painting, which probably wasn't even that good. I had read enough ideas into that pale face to fill a library; I had imbued it with qualities that were not just unlikely, but impossible. But now I had caught her pursuing base pleasures in a gaudy cabaret, like so many other frivolous girls of her generation. The madonna in the bobcat coat, to whom I had accorded such respect, was nothing more than a common *consommatrice*.

I kept a close eye on the boxes, watching the comings and goings; within half an hour I had seen and examined all the passionate couples they contained. Clearly the Madonna in a Fur Coat was not hiding away in one of them. I even went so far as to discreetly peek inside, every time a curtain parted. But I could see no one sitting alone, no couple that had yet to come out to dance.

Once again I lost my nerve. Was the woman I had followed here no more than another vision? She wasn't, after all, the only woman in Berlin in possession of a fur coat. I hadn't even seen her face. Could I really presume to know a woman just from the way she walked? A woman who had done no more than mock me with a smile, having seen me in a drunken stupor? If I had seen her at all. What if I had, in fact, been dreaming this entire day? Gripped by a new fear, I wondered what was happening to me. How and why had this painting come to possess me? To think that I could have believed she was the same woman, passing me by in the dead of night! To think that I had followed her, simply because of her footsteps and her fur coat! There was nothing left for me to do but to leave this place at once, and keep a close eye on myself thereafter.

Just then, the room went dark. There was only a faint light falling on the orchestra. The dance floor emptied out. Soon afterwards came the strains of a slow and solemn melody. Rising from the wind section, I could hear the thin wail of a violin.

Slowly, it grew in volume. A young woman dressed in a white, low-cut dress stepped down onto the dance floor, still playing the violin. In a voice so low it almost sounded like a man's, she began to sing one of the songs that were all the rage then. A projector cast an oval light that followed her across the floor.

I recognized her straight away. The puzzle was solved – and my speculations shattered. Oh, how my heart ached! How sad it was, to see her flashing those false smiles, playing the coquette with such sad reluctance!

I could imagine the woman in the portrait in any number of positions, and even jumping from lap to lap. But nothing could have prepared me for seeing her like this. How miserable she looked! Where was the proud, strong, defiant Madonna of my dreams?

'It would have been better to have seen her as I imagined just a little earlier,' I told myself. 'Getting drunk with men, dancing and kissing them.' Because, if that were the case, then if nothing else she'd be doing so of her own volition. Forgetting herself. Getting carried away. Now, though, I could see very clearly that she had no interest whatsoever in what she was doing. There was nothing extraordinary about the way she played the violin, but her voice was even more beautiful than she was, or rather it had pathos. She sang songs that quivered with longing, as if the words were tumbling out of a drunken boy's mouth. The smile she had fixed on her face – almost like a patch – seemed desperate to escape: when, after leaning to sing a few stale refrains into a customer's ear, she moved on to the next table, her face would grow suddenly stern, reverting to the expression I knew so well from the painting. Nothing grieves me more than seeing someone who has given up on the world being forced to smile. As she approached one table, a drunk young man stood up unsteadily and kissed her bare back. She winced, as if bitten by a snake, but the cold shiver that rippled across her body was gone in a quarter of a second. Turning around, she smiled at the drunkard, as if to say, 'Oh, how lovely!' Then she turned to the woman beside him, who seemed displeased with her companion, nodding as if to say, 'Let it be, madam, this is just how men are. What can we do but indulge them?'

After every song there was applause, and then, with a nod, the woman signalled for the orchestra to play another number. She would begin singing in that voice, that was so thick with indignation, her long white gown sliding across the parquet floor as she went from table to table. Stopping at a table where a drunken couple were embracing, or before the closed curtains of a private box, she would tuck her violin under her chin and run her somewhat clumsy fingers over the strings.

When I saw her approaching my table, I was gripped by a terrible panic. How could I face her? What could I say? Then I laughed at the absurdity of my own questions. Did I really think she was going to recognize a man she had passed in darkness the previous night? What more could I be to her than just a young man who had come here to find fun, with lively companions? All the same, I kept my head lowered. The hem of her gown was covered with dust from being dragged across the floor. Peeking out from underneath it was the tip of an open white shoe. Her foot was bare. In the projector's white glow, I could see a pink impression on the top of her foot, just above her toes. Suddenly I could imagine her before me, entirely undressed. I lifted my head in shame. She was looking at me intently. Not singing, but playing the violin. That false smile was gone. But in her eyes I could read a warm greeting. Yes, I could. Without pretence, and without moving her lips, she was greeting me like an old friend. She spoke only with her eyes, but she made her meaning clear. This time, I knew I wasn't wrong. Then she gave me a smile. A smile that lit up her entire face – open, pure and genuine. She smiled at me like I was an old friend . . . After playing a little more, she nodded once again, and with her eyes bade me farewell, before leaving for another table.

And I was seized by an overwhelming desire to leap up, throw my arms around her, kiss her on the lips and let the tears flow. Never before had I felt such happiness. I could feel my heart opening, as if for the first time. How was it that a person could bring such happiness to another without really doing anything at all? A friendly greeting, an innocent smile . . . and at that moment I wanted nothing else. I was the richest man in the world. As my eyes followed her around the room, I murmured to myself, 'Thank you . . . thank you so much.' For now I knew that I had seen the truth in that painting. She was real, but just as I had imagined. Had it been otherwise, would she ever have recognized me, or greeted me so warmly?

Then a doubt shot through me: I wondered if she had confused me with someone else. Or perhaps (having seen me in that shocking state the night before) she had thought she might know me, and so had greeted me just in case? But I'd not seen any doubt in her eyes, no hesitant search for a connection. She had looked at me in full confidence and then she had smiled. Whatever her intentions, she had, by opening herself up to me, made me the happiest man in the world. So there I sat, beaming with brash confidence, gazing with ease at the goings on around me, and watching the young woman work the room. Her dark wavy bob bouncing against the back of her neck, her bare arms swinging at her sides, and her waist softy swaying as waves rippled across the taut muscles in her back.

When she had finished her last song, she slipped behind the orchestra and vanished. Then the lights came on. For a time I just sat there, lost in thought and jubilation. Then I asked myself what I should do next. Should I leave the place at once and wait for her at the door? But how would I explain myself? I'd not said a word to her, after all. How could I now wait for her and offer to walk her home? What would she think of me, if I did? Why would she want to show me the slightest interest, if I used the trite words of a womanizer?

I decided then that it would be more courteous to leave at once, and return the next night. This would allow our friendship to grow slowly . . . This was already far too much for one night . . . Ever since boyhood, I'd feared wasting any happiness that came my way; I'd always wanted to save some of it for later. This had caused me to miss many opportunities. Even so, I'd always been reluctant to wish for more, lest I frighten away my good fortune.

I scanned the room for the waiter. As my eyes passed over the orchestra, I saw her stepping back into the room. She was no longer holding her violin. She was walking very quickly. When I saw that she was walking in my direction, I looked around to see who might be waiting for her. She was coming to my table, coming to me. With the same friendly smile. Stopping at my table, she held out her hand: 'How are you?' she said.

Somehow, I managed to overcome my surprise. I jumped to my feet.

'Thank you . . . I'm fine.'

She sat down on the stool opposite me. Smoothing back her hair, she looked me straight in the eye. 'Are you angry with me?'

What could she mean? Frantically, I searched my addled mind. 'Angry?' I said. 'No, of course not.'

How familiar her voice was! This must be because I was so intimately acquainted with every line in her face and could read between them.

My long inspections of the painting had engraved it onto my mind. I had further strengthened the impression by studying the original. But her voice . . . most likely I had heard it before. Somewhere . . . maybe long ago, in my childhood . . . maybe only in my imagination.

I shifted in my seat. Enough! I told myself. She was here, at my table. She was speaking to me. This was not the time for silly games.

Again, she asked me: 'You aren't angry with me, then? So why didn't you ever come back?'

Dear God! She really *had* confused me with someone else . . . I opened my mouth, to ask her how she knew me. But then I stopped myself. This was not the right thing to ask. What if she took it the wrong way? She might make her excuses, and get up and leave.

Best to prolong this dream, this miracle, for as long as I could. What was I to gain by cutting it short? Soon enough, I would wake up to the truth.

When she saw I wasn't going to answer her question, she changed her tack: 'Does your mother write to you?'

Electrified by shock, I leapt from my chair. Taking her hands in mine, I cried: 'Oh, my God, it was you?' And suddenly it all made sense. At last, I knew where I'd recognized her voice.

She let out a light, bright laugh: 'You really are a strange young man.'

I recognized that laugh, too. She'd laughed the same way when she'd joined me on the bench across from the painting, and asked me what I thought of it, and when I said that the woman in the painting reminded me of my mother, she'd let out that same laugh and asked me if I had a picture of my mother . . . What I could not understand was how I'd failed to recognize her at the time. Had that painting hypnotized me? Had it blinded me to the real world?

'But you, you didn't look anything like the painting at the time,' I murmured.

'How do you know that?' she said. 'You didn't even look at my face.'

'No, I believe that I did . . . How can that be?'

'You did glance up at me once or twice . . . but do you want to know how? As if you didn't want to see me.'

She pulled away her hands: 'When I went back over to my friends, I didn't tell them that you hadn't recognized me. Otherwise they would have laughed at you.'

'Thank you.'

She thought for a moment, and a cloud settled in her eyes; suddenly she was serious. 'So, do you still want to have a mother like that?'

For a moment I was unable to remember. Then my words tumbled out. 'Of course . . . of course . . . so very much.'

'That's just what you said then.'

'Perhaps . . .'

She smiled again. 'But how could I be your mother?'

'Oh, no, no . . .'

'Maybe your sister!'

'How old are you?'

'Now how can you ask a question like that? All the same, I'm twenty-six . . . you?'

'Twenty-four.'

'You see? I could be your sister.'

'Yes . . .'

We were silent for a while. I had so much to say to her, enough to fill whole years or an eternity . . . but at that moment, I couldn't think of a single word. She, too, was looking blankly into the distance, her right elbow propped up on the table, and her hand casually draped across the white tablecloth. The tips of her long, fine, tapered fingers were flushed red, as if from cold. And now I remembered how cold her hands felt. Seizing the advantage, I said: 'Your hands are so very cold.'

She answered without hesitation. 'Warm them up.' And she held them out to me.

I looked into her face. Her gaze was bold and strong-willed. It was almost as if she found nothing extraordinary about surrendering her hands to a man with whom she was conversing for the first time. Unless? Again, my mind spun with ugly possibilities. So I began to speak, in the hope that this would chase my fears away: 'I hope you will forgive me for failing to recognize you at the exhibition,' I said. 'It's just that you were so cheerful. You even teased me . . . and then, how can I put this, you were nothing like the woman in the painting . . . you had short hair . . . a short skirt and such a tight coat . . . When you rushed off, you were nearly skipping . . . It would have been difficult to see you in that wise, thoughtful, even mournful painting that the critics dubbed the Madonna . . . Even so, I have to wonder . . . I must have been lost in thought.'

'Yes, very much so . . . I remember the first day you came to the exhibition. You were strolling through the gallery looking rather bored, when you suddenly stopped in front of my portrait. You looked at it so strangely! Everyone around you noticed. For a moment I thought you must have likened me to someone you knew. Then you started coming every day . . . So naturally I was curious. Now and again, I joined you. We'd sit there together, looking at the painting. But still you didn't recognize me, even though you'd turn your head from time to time, to glance at this stranger who was ruining your concentration. There was something oddly appealing about the way you just sat there, lost in thought . . . Like I said, I was curious . . . Then one day I went over and talked to you. My artist friends were as curious about you as I was . . . it was their idea . . . But I wish I hadn't . . . because after that I lost you altogether . . . you raced out of the gallery, and never came back.'

'I thought you were making fun of me,' I said. Immediately I regretted it, fearing she might take offence. Instead, she said: 'Well, you were right.'

She searched my face. 'You are alone in Berlin, right?'

'What do you mean?'

'I mean . . . alone . . . with no one else . . . spiritually alone . . . How can I put it . . . you have such an air about you that . . .'

'I understand . . . I am completely alone . . . But not just in Berlin . . . alone in all of the world . . . since I was a child . . .'

'Me too,' she said. This time she took my hands in hers. 'So alone sometimes I feel like I can't breathe . . . as lonely as a sick dog.'

Squeezing my hands even tighter, she lifted them up. Then she pounded the table with her fist. 'We could be friends,' she cried. 'You're just getting to know me, but I have been observing you for nearly twenty days . . . There is something special about you . . . Yes, we would make excellent friends.'

Bewildered, I looked into her eyes. What was she trying to say? What could a woman offer a man in a situation such as mine? I had no idea. I had no experience and knew nothing about people.

She could see that. And I could see her concern. Fearing she had gone too far, or said something I might take the wrong way, she said: 'Now don't you dare start thinking like all the other men . . . I don't want you reading volumes into everything I say . . . just know that I am always completely open . . . like this . . . like a man . . . I'm like a man in many other ways, too. Maybe that's why I'm alone . . .'

She looked me over, before exclaiming: 'And you're a bit like a woman! I can see it now. Maybe that's why I've liked you ever since I first set eyes on you . . . Yes, indeed. There's something about you that makes me think of a young girl . . .'

How surprised I was – and how saddened – to hear a new acquaintance echo my parents' words!

'I'll never forget the way you looked last night,' she continued. 'Every time I think of it, I laugh. You were wriggling like a young girl struggling to defend her honour. But it's no easy feat, escaping the clutches of Frau van Tiedemann.'

I opened my eyes wide in surprise: 'Do you know her?'

'How could I not? We're related. She's my cousin. But we're not on good terms . . . Actually, it has nothing to do with me . . . it's my mother who's severed relations, because of the way she's been behaving. Her husband was a lawyer. He died in the war. Now she leads a life that Mother finds "unsuitable" . . . but that's none of our business. What happened last night? Did you manage to escape? How do you know each other?'

'We are staying in the same *pension*. But I had a lucky escape. She's close to another resident in the *pension* – Herr Döppke. We ran into him in the corridor.'

'They might as well get married.'

From the way she uttered these words, it was clear that she wished to say no more on the subject. For a time, we were silent. But we were still trying to look each other over, without making it too obvious, and whenever our eyes met, we smiled, liking what we saw.

I was the first to break the silence: 'So you have a mother then?'

'Yes! Just like you!'

I wanted to kick myself for having asked such a silly question. Noticing, she changed the subject. 'It's the first time I've seen you here.'

'Yes, I've never been to a place like this . . . but tonight . . .'

'Tonight?'

Mustering all my courage, I said: 'I followed you here.'

That seemed to surprise her. 'Were you the one that followed me all the way to the door?'

'Yes. So you noticed?'

'Of course . . . How could a woman not notice such a thing?'

'But you never looked over your shoulder.'

'I never look back . . .'

Again, we fell silent. She was mulling something over, I could see. Then she looked up, smiling mischievously. 'It's just a game I play. If I think someone's following me, I don't let my curiosity get the better of me. I never turn my head. Instead, I run through all the possibilities. Is my pursuer a young man, or a feeble old man who likes his women young? Is he a rich prince? A penniless student? A homeless drunkard? I try to guess, judging by their footsteps, and before I know it I've arrived! . . . So, then, it was you tonight? But your footsteps were so hesitant. I took you for an old man. Old and married.'

Now she looked into my eyes: 'So you waited for me on the street?'

'Yes.'

'How did you know I would pass that same spot? Did you know that I worked here?'

'No, how would I know that? I thought that maybe . . . Indeed, I didn't think, but rather I found myself in the very same place at the same hour. Then I was afraid you might see me. So I hid in a doorway.'

'Come on, let's go . . . we can talk on the way . . .'

Seeing my surprise, she asked: 'Don't you want to walk me home?'

I leapt up from my seat. This made her laugh.

'There's no rush, my friend,' she said, 'I still need to change out of this dress. Wait for me at the door. I'll be out in five minutes.'

Rising to her feet, she lifted up her dress and skipped away. Just before she vanished behind the orchestra pit, she turned around, fixing me with those magnificent eyes of hers. Winking, as if we had been friends for forty years.

I beckoned to the waiter and asked for the bill. Suddenly I felt light-hearted, even brave. As I watched the waiter standing there, totting up the figures, I had the overwhelming urge to smile and say, 'Just look how happy I am, you fools!' I wanted to salute every customer in the room, throw my arms around them all, even the musicians, and embrace them like long-lost friends.

Rising, I strode off to the cloakroom. Though I normally disdained such gestures, I gave a mark to the woman who handed me my coat. Outside, I took a deep breath and looked around me. They had turned off the electricity. The sign above the door was no longer lit. I could see neither the waves nor the letters spelling out 'ATLANTIC'. The sky was clear and there was a sliver of a crescent moon on the western horizon.

Behind me I heard a low voice: 'Have you been waiting long?'

'No, I just came out now,' I said, turning around.

She was standing across from me, blinking like someone who was struggling to make up her mind. Then finally she said: 'You seem like a good person.'

But by now my courage had deserted me. Though I longed to thank her, and take her hands in mine, and kiss her, I only managed a low whisper. 'Really? I don't know.'

With disarming confidence, she took my arm. Cupping my chin in her other hand, she spoke to me in the sort of voice you'd use to soothe a child: 'Oh, you really are innocent, aren't you? As pure as a little girl.'

Blushing furiously, I cast my eyes down. I did not like being addressed so casually by a woman. Thankfully she didn't go any further. Letting go of my chin and releasing my arm, she let her own arms fall by her side. When at last I raised my eyes, I saw, with some amazement, that she looked shocked, even ashamed. Her cheeks were flushed, and her neck too. Her eyes were half closed, as if she hardly dared to look at me. A question instantly came to mind: 'Why is she behaving like this? Clearly, she is not that kind of woman . . . But then, why is she behaving like this?'

She seemed to read my mind. 'That's just the way I am,' she said. 'I'm a strange woman . . . and if you want to be my friend, you're going to have to get used to quite a lot. My little caprices, my awkward working hours . . . I have to warn you – my friends have always found me to be an unsettling and exasperating creature . . .'

Then, as if she were angry for being so hard on herself, she assumed a tone of voice that was sharp to the point of rudeness: 'But suit yourself . . . I don't need friends, and I don't seek them out . . . I don't want to depend on the kindness of others. I am beholden to no one . . . so it's up to you . . .'

When I spoke, it was in my usual, fearful voice: 'I'll try to understand you.' We walked in silence for a time. Slipping her arm around mine, she began to talk. Her voice was flat, as if we were chatting about matters of no importance.

'So you're going to try to understand me? That's not a bad idea . . . but I'm warning you, it might be in vain. Only sometimes do I think that I might actually make a good friend. Time will tell. If I draw you into petty arguments from time to time, don't pay too much attention. Don't take it personally.'

Stopping in the middle of the street, she wagged her finger at me, as if she were telling a child to behave: 'There's one thing you must remember. This all ends the moment you want something from me. You can't ask me for anything . . . Anything – do you hear?' It was almost as if she were arguing with a faceless enemy, for now, as she continued, her voice was thick with anger. 'Do you know why I hate you? You and every other man in the world? Because you ask so much of us, as if it were your natural right . . . Mark my words, for it can happen without a single word being uttered . . . it's how men look at us and smile at us. It's how they raise their hands. To put it simply, it's how they treat us . . . you'd have to be blind not to see how much confidence they have, and how stupidly they achieve it. And if you need a measure of their arrogant pride, all you need is to see how shocked they are when an advance is rejected. They are the hunters, you see. And we their miserable prey. And our duties? To bow down and obey, and give them whatever they want . . . But we shouldn't. We shouldn't give away a single bit of ourselves. It's revolting, this arrogant male pride . . . Do you understand what I'm saying? Yes, well, that's why I think that maybe we can be friends. Because I can't see a trace of that awful male pride in you . . . but I don't know . . . even when he has a lamb between his teeth, a wolf can hide his savagery behind a smile . . .'

Somewhere in the middle of her speech, we had started walking again. Walking fast, while she gesticulated angrily, gazing now at the ground and now at the sky. She would stop mid sentence, as if she had said all there was to say. Then narrowing her eyes, she'd walk on.

We carried on like this for some time. And then once again we fell into a long silence. I walked beside her, in fearful silence, until she stopped in front of a three-storey stone building on one of the streets near the Tiergarten.

'This is where I live . . . with my mother,' she said. 'We can continue this conversation tomorrow . . . But don't come to the club . . . I don't think I would be happy for you to see me like that again . . . Consider that a point in your favour . . . Let's meet tomorrow during the day . . . we can take a stroll together.

I can show you some of my favourite places in Berlin. Let's see what you think of them. So for now goodnight . . . Just a minute: I still don't know your name!'

'Raif.'

'Raif? Is that all?'

'Hatip zade Raif.'

'Oh, that's impossible . . . how could I ever remember that? I can't even pronounce it. Could I just say Raif?'

'That would make me even happier.'

'And you can just call me Maria . . . like I say, I don't want to feel beholden.'

She smiled again and though she had changed expression many times since we'd met, she now wore the sweet face of a friend. She reached out and squeezed my hand. In a gentle, almost apologetic voice, she said goodnight, before pulling out her keys and turning away. Slowly I walked off. I had taken no more than ten steps when I heard her calling out to me.

'Raif!'

I turned around and waited.

'Come back! Come back!' It sounded as if she were trying to stop herself from laughing. And then, assuming an elaborately courteous tone, she said: 'I'm delighted that we're already on first-name terms.' She was talking to me from the top of the stairs, so I looked up to see her. But it was too dark to see a thing. I waited for her to go on. She still seemed on the verge of laughter, while struggling to stay serious. 'So you're going, then?'

My heart skipped a beat. I took a step forward. Would I be glad to have stayed? I was unable to decide. But as much as my mind rejected it, hope found its way through. 'Should I stay?'

She came down two steps. Her face was now lit by the street lamp. Those dark eyes looked sly now, and curious. 'So you still don't know why I called you back?'

Oh yes, I knew . . . I was coming back to hurl myself into her arms. But at the same time I felt a powerful sense of loss, shock, even nausea. Flushing, I looked down at the ground. No, No! I didn't want it to be like this.

She was running her hand across my cheek. 'What's happening to you? You look as if you're about to cry. You really do need a mother and not just a sister . . . So, tell me, you were really just about to leave?'

'Yes.'

'You aren't going to look for me in the Atlantic again . . . that's what we agreed.'

'Yes. Tomorrow we can meet during the day.'

'Where?'

I stared at her stupidly. I hadn't thought of that. In a plaintive little voice, I asked: 'Is that why you called me back?'

'Of course . . . You really are nothing like other men . . . The first thing they do is make sure they have everything pinned down. You just up and leave . . . The person you're seeking doesn't always just pop up wherever you want them to be, like tonight.'

Now a terrible doubt overtook me. I wondered, fearfully, if all that lay ahead was an ordinary affair. I could never agree to that. I could never see the Madonna in a Fur Coat in that way. I would rather be dismissed as foolish and immature. Even so, the very thought made me sad . . . I imagined her laughing behind my back after I'd left – mocking my innocence and lack of courage. I imagined myself losing hope in everyone and everything and cutting myself off from the world for ever.

But now my mind was at ease. How ashamed I was, to have entertained such impudent suspicions! How grateful I was to the friend who had chased them away! Drawing upon reserves I'd not known I had, I said, 'You are an exceptional woman.'

'Don't rush to conclusions . . . With someone like me, you need to be cautious.'

I took her hands in mine and kissed them. Most probably tears were welling up in my eyes. For a moment she came closer, almost close enough to embrace. Seeing the warm glow in her eyes, I thought my heart might stop. Heaven was only centimetres away. But then, suddenly stern, she pulled her hands away and stood up straight. 'Where do you live?'

'On Lützow Street.'

'So you aren't far from here . . . Why don't you come and pick me up here tomorrow afternoon.'

'Which apartment do you live in?'

'I'll wait for you at the window. There's no need for you to come up.'

Turning the key in the door, she stepped inside.

This time I hurried away quickly. My body had never felt lighter. I was guided by her image. I was murmuring something under my breath. What was it? Paying closer attention, I realized that I was saying her name over and over, and caressing her with sweet words. From time to time I couldn't help myself and let out a quiet little laugh. By the time I'd reached the *pension* it was almost dawn.

For the first time since childhood, I drifted off to sleep without meditating on the meaningless of existence and despairing of the day just passed, which had been no more than a repetition of the one before, and had led nowhere.

The next day I stayed away from the factory. Towards half past two in the afternoon I made my way through the Tiergarten to Maria Puder's apartment. I wondered if I was too early. I was reluctant to disturb her, knowing how tired she would be, after working so late into the night. My compassion for her knew no bounds. I imagined her lying in her bed, her hair spread out across her pillow, her breathing slow and deep, and it seemed to me that there could be no greater vision of happiness.

All my life, I'd kept my heart closed. I had never known love. But now, all at once, the doors had flown open. My unspent passions had been released, to illuminate this one magnificent woman.

I was only too aware that I still knew next to nothing about her. My judgements were formed of my own dreams and illusions. At the same time, I was absolutely sure that they would not deceive me.

All my life, I'd been waiting for her. Searching for her. Scanning my surroundings for some sign of her. Bitter experience had given me second sight, and had it ever been wrong? Too often I had allowed reason and experience to cloud my judgement, for my first impressions were largely correct. I'd tell myself I had been too quick to judge. I'd make allowances, only to discover, sooner or later, that I'd been right in the first place, and wrong to have been swayed by external factors.

Now Maria Puder was someone for whom I could set no conditions or requirements, if I was to live. At first it felt strange to accept this. How could I long so for someone whose existence I'd only just become aware of? But wasn't it always like this? Some things we never know we need until we find them. And now, when I looked back on my life, it seemed empty and idle, if only because she'd not been in it. All my life, I'd shied away from human company, never sharing my thoughts with a soul. How pointless this seemed now, and how absurd! I'd thought that it was life itself that had ground me down – that my sadness stemmed from spiritual malaise. After spending two hours with a book, and finding it more pleasurable than two years of real life, I'd remember again that life had no meaning, and sink back into despair.

But since first setting eyes on that painting, everything had changed. I'd lived more during the past two weeks than in all the years of my life put together. Every day, every hour, was full, even when I was asleep. It was not just my tired limbs that were coming to life. It was also my soul, revealing to me the sublime vista it had kept buried for so long. Maria Puder had taught me I had a soul. And now, overcoming a habit of a lifetime, I could see a soul in her. Of course, everyone else in the world was similarly endowed. But most would come into this world and leave it without even knowing what they had missed. A soul only came forward when it found its twin, when it felt no need to rely on mere words to explain itself . . . It was only then that we truly began to live – live with our soul. At that moment, all doubts and shame could be set aside. All rules could be broken, as two souls joined in embrace. All my inhibitions had disappeared. All I wanted was to pour out my heart to her, the good with the bad, the weaknesses with the strengths, holding nothing back, baring my soul. I had so much to say to her . . . enough to fill a lifetime. All my life, I'd been silent. Whenever I'd been tempted to speak, I'd quickly changed my mind. 'Why bother?' I'd say to myself. 'What difference will it make if you speak?' In the past, I'd been just as quick to let emotion get in the way – to decide, on slim evidence, that a certain person could never understand me. But this time, my first impressions stood fast: *she* would understand me perfectly.

Skirting the southern side of the Tiergarten, I took my time, finally arriving at a canal. I could see Maria Puder's house from the bridge. It had only just gone three. The sun was shimmering on the windowpanes: I couldn't make out anyone behind them. So I leaned against the railing on the bridge and looked down at the still waters. Soon those same waters were quivering in a haze of raindrops. In the far distance, a barge was unloading fruit and vegetables, while a row of handcarts waited on the pier. Leaves fell from the trees that lined the canal, drawing spirals through the air. So much beauty in this dark and dreary scene! Oh, to breathe in this moist air! This was how life should be lived: attuned to nature, its every flutter and sway, while time moves inexorably forward. Rejoicing in every moment, finding a lifetime in each and every one, in the knowledge that these moments were revealing themselves to me as to no other. Never forgetting that there existed another with whom I could share all my thoughts. I just had to wait . . .

What could be more uplifting than this? Soon we would be wandering down these wet roads together. Finding a dark and quiet place to sit down. Locking eyes. I had so much to tell her – things I had never even admitted to myself. Thoughts that had arrived only to flit away a moment later, to make room for the next. I would take her hands in mine and rub them warm. I would, with just one word, be at one with her.

It was nearly half past three. I wondered if she was awake yet. Would it be right to go straight over to her house and wait there? She'd told me she'd look for me from the window. Would she guess I was waiting over here? Was she really planning to join me? I drove the doubt from my mind. Just to ask such a question betrayed a lack of trust, which was undeserved: I had built up an idea of her, only to want to kick it down. But now I was assailed by a thousand possibilities. Perhaps she had fallen ill. Perhaps she had already left the house on pressing business. That had to be it. It wasn't natural for happiness to arrive so suddenly. With every passing minute, my panic increased. My heart began to race. It happened only once in a lifetime – a night like that. It couldn't be right to expect another. I was already looking for ways to console myself. I might have been unwise, I told myself, to take my life down a new path. For all

I could see there was darkness. Wouldn't it be easier to return to my old silence, my old numbing routine?

I turned to see her walking towards me. She was wearing a thin raincoat, a lavender beret, low, heeled shoes, and a smile. She held out her hand.

'Is this where you've been waiting for me? How long have you been here?'

'An hour.'

My voice was trembling. Taking this as a complaint, she teased me with a reproach: 'You're the one to blame for that, sir. I've been waiting for the last hour and a half. It was only just now that I managed to spot you. And then only by chance. It seems that you preferred to stay here, enjoying the poetry of nature, instead of coming to stand in front of my building!'

So she *had* been waiting for me. Which meant I was important to her. I looked into her eyes. I might have been a kitten, being stroked: 'Thank you.'

'Why are you thanking me?'

Then she put her arm in mine before I could answer: 'Come on, let's go.'

With that, I surrendered myself. We set off at a brisk pace. I was afraid to ask where we were going. Neither of us spoke. And how I savoured that silence, even as I ate myself up, racking my brain for something to say. But my beautiful thoughts had deserted me. The more I searched for them, the more my mind emptied out, until it was nothing more than a throbbing, piteous piece of meat. But when I glanced over at her, I saw not a trace of agitation. She had her dark eyes fixed on the ground before her. Though stonily silent, there was the hint of a smile as she let her left hand fall on my arm. With her right hand she seemed to be pointing at something in the distance.

I looked up at her face again. Her thick, wild eyebrows were furrowed. She was mulling something over. I could see thin blue veins in her eyelids. Her long black eyelashes were quivering, as tiny droplets of rain glimmered on their tips. Her hair was getting wet.

Suddenly turning, she asked: 'Why are you staring at me?'

I had already asked myself the same question: how could I gaze at a woman with such open ease, when I had never done so before? And why, even after she had challenged me, was I bold enough to persist? I was even able to say: 'Don't you want me to look?'

'No, it's not that, I was just asking . . . Maybe I do want you to. Maybe that's why I'm asking.'

She looked at me meaningfully. Unable to bear the force of those dark eyes, I asked: 'Are you originally German?'

'Yes, why do you ask?'

'You aren't blonde and you haven't got blue eyes.'

'True enough.'

Again, she almost smiled, but this time I sensed some hesitation.

'My father was Jewish,' she said. 'My mother is German. But she's not blonde either.'

Curious, I asked: 'So that means you're Jewish?'

'Yes . . . but I hope you don't mind my asking. Are you an enemy of the Jews?'

'Nothing of the sort . . . we don't harbour that kind of animosity. But it hadn't occurred to me that you might be Jewish.'

'Yes, I'm Jewish. My father is from Prague. But he converted to Catholicism before I was even born.'

'So you would call yourself Christian.'

'No . . . I have nothing to do with religion.'

We walked for some time. She had stopped talking. I had no more questions for her. Slowly we made our way to the outskirts of the city. I was beginning to wonder just where we were going. I didn't suppose she'd be taking me on a country walk in this weather. The rain was still falling, at the same rate as before. At one point Maria said: 'Where are we going?'

'I don't know.'

'Aren't you curious?'

'I'll go wherever you take me . . . Wherever you like.'

She turned to look at me. Her pale, moist face was like a white flower covered in dew: 'How obedient you are . . . don't you have any ideas of your own? Any desires?'

I reminded her of what she'd said the night before: 'You forbade me to ask anything of you.'

She fell silent. I waited a few moments, before continuing: 'Or didn't you mean what you said last night? Or maybe you've changed your mind?'

'No, no!' she cried, with some vehemence. 'I meant every word . . .'

Then she fell back into thought. We had come to the front of a large garden surrounded by an iron fence.

'Shall we go inside?'

'What is this place?'

'A botanical garden.'

'It's up to you.'

'Well then, let's go in . . . I always come here. Especially on rainy days like this.'

There was no one inside. We spent some time wandering along the sandy paths. Despite the advanced season, they were lined on both sides by trees that still had their leaves. We passed ponds ringed by moss-flecked rocks and grassy banks and flowers of all colours. Large leaves floated on the surface of the water. Inside vaulting greenhouses were plants and trees from warmer climates. Gazing at their thick trunks and tiny leaves,

Maria said: 'This is the most beautiful place in Berlin. There are hardly any visitors at this time of year. It's practically empty . . . and then these strange trees always remind me of all the faraway lands I long to see . . . I pity them, you know – for having been uprooted from their natural soil and brought here to be grown under artificial conditions, with such exacting care. Did you know that Berlin has only a hundred days of sun a year, and the remaining two hundred and sixty-five days are overcast? Can hothouses and artificial lighting ever be enough for leaves accustomed to so much heat and light? Somehow they survive. They manage not to wither away . . . but can we call this life? To take a living plant from its natural environment, and keep it in such awful confinement, just so a few enthusiasts can enjoy them . . . isn't that a kind of torture?'

'But aren't you one of those enthusiasts?'

'Yes, but every time I come here, I leave feeling desperately sad.'

'Then why do you come at all?'

'I don't know.'

She sat down on a wet bench. I sat down beside her. Wiping the raindrops off her face, she said: 'When I look at these plants, I end up thinking about myself a bit. Maybe they remind me of my ancestors, who lived in the same lands as these strange flowers and trees many centuries ago. Because weren't we uprooted, just like they were? Banished from our lands, and sent to wander the world? They can't mean the same to you, though . . . Truth is, they don't mean that much to me . . . it's just that they give the chance to think, and to imagine. You'll see – I live more in my head than anywhere else. In comparison, my real life is a dull dream . . . You might find my work at the Atlantic depressing, but I myself have no fixed opinion . . . In fact, I sometimes even find it amusing . . . In any case, I took on the job because of my mother. I have to look after her and there is no way for me to support us on a few paintings a year . . . Have you ever tried your hand at painting?'

'Just for a while!'

'Why did you stop?'

'I saw that I had no talent.'

'That's not possible . . . just from the way you were looking at the paintings in the gallery, I could tell that you do . . . Now you might have said that you saw that you lacked the courage. But it's not done, is it, for a man to admit to such a thing . . . I'm talking about you now. Because I do have the courage. I want to make paintings that express how I see people, and sometimes I may even be successful. But that, too, is meaningless . . . There is no way for those I scorn to understand what I've done, while those who do understand are in any event above scorn. By this I mean to say that painting, like all arts, answers to no one – it falls short of its aspirations. In spite of which it is the most important thing I do. That is why – that is the only reason why – I do not wish to live off my paintings. Because then I wouldn't be doing what I wanted, but what people wanted of me . . . never . . . never . . . I would rather sell my body on the street . . . because for me, it has no importance . . .'

She punched my knee hard. 'And so that's the way it is, my dear friend. In the end, we're no different. You were there last night when that drunkard kissed my back, weren't you? Why wouldn't he . . . he has every right . . . he's spending money . . . and they say that my back is very enticing . . . Would you like to kiss it, too? Do you have the money?'

I sat there, tongue-tied. I was blinking furiously and biting my lips. Noticing this, Maria frowned. Her face seemed paler than ever. 'No, Raif, I don't want it . . . anything but this . . . If there's one thing I cannot bear, it's pity . . . The moment I see you pitying me is the moment I say goodbye . . . you'll never see my face again . . .'

Seeing how shocked I was – seeing that I was the one to be pitied just then, she put her hand on my shoulder. 'Don't take this personally,' she said. 'It's just that we shouldn't shy away from speaking openly about things that could hurt our relationship later. It's at times like this that cowardice can be damaging . . . What will come of it? If we find we cannot get along, then we'll just say goodbye and go our separate ways . . . Where's the tragedy in that? The essence of life is in solitude – wouldn't you agree? All unions are built on falsehood. People can only get to know each other up to a point and then they make up the rest, until one day, seeing their mistake, they turn their backs on sadness and run away. Would this ever happen, if they stopped believing in their dreams and made do with what was possible? If everyone accepted what was natural, then no one would suffer disappointment, no one would curse fate. We have every right to see our situation as pitiful, but we must confine our pity to ourselves. To pity another is to assume superiority and that is why we must never think we are superior to others, or that others are more unfortunate . . . Shall we go?'

We both stood up. We shook the raindrops off our coats. The wet sand crunched under our feet.

Night was falling, but the street lamps were not yet lit. We walked quickly by the route we had come. This time I linked my arm with hers. Like a little child I snuggled up to her, my head close to hers, my elation tinged with sadness. For as happy as I was that we thought so similarly, and were already so close, I was afraid – that one day she would leave me or hide the truth from me. That we would never, whatever the cost, agree to live a lie. And from somewhere deep inside, I could hear a faint voice warning me: once you have seen someone as she truly is – once you have accepted reality stripped bare – it doesn't matter who she is: intimacy is no longer possible.

Whereas I had no desire to see reality stripped bare. Because I knew that I would never be able to bear any truth that might take me away from her. We had found in each other rare treasures. Would it not be more humane to show each other some mercy, turning a blind eye to the details, sacrificing the smaller truths for the greater?

Here was a woman of sound judgement, offering hard-won advice. She had been through hard times, and seen those around her damaged. Naturally she would think this way. She deeply resented having to live in company she had not chosen, and did not like. A life of forced smiles had made her suspicious. Whereas I had kept my distance from others all my life. I had not bothered them, and they had not bothered me, and so I harboured no anger. It was only my loneliness that ate at me, and it was this same loneliness that led me to betray myself in myriad ways.

We had come to the city centre. The streets were brightly lit and crowded. Maria Puder was lost in thought and perhaps a little sad. Fearfully I asked: 'Is something bothering you?'

'No,' she replied. 'Nothing happened today that bothered me. In fact I'm happy about this walk we just took. At least, I suppose I'm happy . . .'

It was clear that her mind was elsewhere. Her eyes seemed almost to look through me. And her smile had a strange and unnerving edge to it. At one point she stopped in the middle of the street and said: 'I don't want to go home. Come on, let's get something to eat. We can keep talking until it's time for me to go to work.'

I jumped at this unexpected offer. Seeing her alarm at my show of enthusiasm, I quickly collected myself. We went on to a sizeable restaurant on the western side of the city. It was not particularly crowded. Playing loudly in a corner was a Bavarian female band dressed in traditional attire. We sat down at a table and ordered food and wine.

By now my companion's low spirits had passed on to me. I felt bored and restless without knowing why. Noticing my change in mood, she tried to wrestle free of her thoughts and open up a little. With a smile, she leaned across the table and slapped my hand: 'Why the glum face? A young man enjoying his first supper with a young woman should make more of an effort!' The tone of her voice was light, but it was clear that she didn't believe what she was saying. And soon she had slipped back into her own thoughts. Just to busy herself in some way, she ran her eyes over the other tables. After taking a few sips of wine, she turned around to look at me. 'What can I do? What? That's the thing – I just can't be any other way!'

What was she trying to say? I could not help interpreting it as something dark. Whatever it was that she couldn't do, it was what was making me sad. That much I knew. But there my understanding ended.

Wherever her eyes settled, she seemed to have difficulty prising them away. From time to time I could see a slight shiver passing across her face, which was as pale as mother of pearl. She started to speak again. There was a quivering in her voice now, as if she were trying to hold back her excitement: 'Whatever you do, don't take offence. It's better to be completely open – so much better than losing yourself in empty hopes . . . But please, don't take offence . . . Last night I came over to you . . . I asked you to walk me home . . . I invited you to come out with me today . . . I said, let's have dinner together . . . I've not left you alone . . . But I don't love you. I've known this since the beginning . . . so no, I don't love you . . . What can I do? I find you pleasant, even attractive, and I see in you qualities I've never seen in another man, but that's all . . . Talking to you, talking to you about everything under the sun, bickering and quarrelling . . . getting cross and then making peace, all these things will make me happy . . . But love? That's beyond me . . . Now you may well ask why I'm saying all this out of the blue . . . so let me say again that I don't want you to build up your hopes, only to take offence later on. I need to make it clear to you what I can and cannot give you, because if I don't you'll accuse me later of playing games with you. As different as you are, you're still a man . . . and all the men that I have ever known have ended up leaving in sorrow or anger once they realize I don't love them, and can never love them . . . But why, when they say goodbye, do they assume I am the one to blame? Because I never gave them what I promised I never would, or because they convinced themselves it would be otherwise? Isn't that unfair? I don't want you to think the same way about me . . . You can consider that a point in your favour . . .'

Her words shocked me. Trying not to lose my composure, I said: 'What is the need for all this? It's you, not me, setting the terms of our friendship. However you want it to be, that's how it will be.'

Angrily she protested: 'No, no, that won't do at all. Look, don't you understand? You're acting like all the other men – acting as if you accept my terms, so as to gain approval. No, my friend! You can't talk this away with fine words. Think about it. I've tried to be open and candid, even if it works against me, even if it works against others. But I am getting nowhere. Men and women have such a hard time understanding what we want from each other, and our emotions are so foggy that we hardly know what we are doing. We get lost in the current. I don't want that. If I have to do things that seem to me to be unnecessary and unsatisfying, I end up hating myself . . . But what I hate most is women always having to be passive . . . Why? Why are we always the ones running away and you are the ones chasing after us? Why is it always that we surrender and you take the spoils? Why is it that even in the way you beg, there is dominance, and pity in the way we refuse? I've been challenging this since childhood. I've never accepted it, ever. Why am I like that? Why is it so important to me, when other women hardly seem to notice? I've thought about this a lot. I've often asked myself if I was abnormal. But no, on the contrary, I've come to think that I'm the normal one. Simply because I grew up far removed from the influences that make most women come to accept their fate. My father died when I was still very young. It was just me and my mother at home. She was the quintessential submissive woman. She had lost the ability to go through life alone, or rather she had never acquired it in the first place. From the age of seven, I was the one in charge. I was the one who guided, advised and supported her. There was no man standing over us. And so naturally I was repulsed by my classmates' idle fantasies. I never learned – or wanted to learn – how to make boys like me. I never blushed when I was around them or fished for compliments. This caused me to become hideously isolated. My girlfriends had a hard time finding things in common with me. They had no interest in being real people: they preferred to be objects of desire and act like dolls. I couldn't make friends with boys either. They'd look for a soft centre and when they saw it wasn't there, when they saw I was a match for them, they'd run away. That's how I understand only too well where men get their strength and ambition; there is no other creature on this earth that races after such easy success, and no other creature as proud, arrogant and egotistical, yet at the same time cowardly and set in his ways. Once I became aware of all of this, it was impossible for me to truly love men. Even the ones I liked the most, and with whom I had the most in common – the moment would arrive when some minor provocation had them baring their wolfish teeth; after being together, and giving each other an equal amount of pleasure, they'd sidle up to me, sighing idiotically, and either apologize or offer to protect me, making it clear that in their eyes, they had vanquished me . . . But they were in fact the ones who had exposed just how pitiful and miserable they really were. There is no woman as pitiful and ridiculous as a man swept away by his passions. At the same time they take huge pride in them, seeing them as proof of their virility. My God, it's enough to drive a person crazy . . . Although I know that there is in me no tendency towards the unnatural, I would rather fall in love with a woman.'

She stopped and looked into my face. Then she drank a little wine. Her monologue seemed to have chased away her dark mood.

'Why do you look so surprised?' she asked. 'Don't worry. It's not what you think. Though I wish I could be like that. Certainly I could have done something that cheapened the soul less . . . It's just that I'm a artist, as you know . . . I have my own standards of beauty . . . I don't think it would be beautiful to make love to a woman . . . How can I put it . . . the aesthetics would be all wrong . . . and then, I am a lover of the natural world . . . I have always been reluctant to behave in a way that goes against the natural world . . . This is why I believe that I definitely need to love a man . . . but a real man . . . a man who could sweep me off my feet without resorting to brute strength . . . without asking anything of me, without controlling me, or degrading me, a man who could love me and walk by my side . . . In other words, a truly powerful man, a real man . . . Now do you see why I can't love you? In any case it hasn't been long enough for that, but you're not the person I'm looking for . . . the truth is you have none of the pride I was just talking about . . . you are so much like a child, or rather a woman. A woman like my mother – you need someone to look after you . . . I could be that person . . . if you wanted . . . but nothing more . . . We could be wonderful friends . . . you are the first man who hasn't interrupted me, or tried to pull me away from my ideas, or tried to bring me round. What I mean is, you're the first man who's listened to what I have to say, without once trying to discipline me . . . I can see in your eyes that you understand me . . . Like I said, we could be great friends. In the same way that I am speaking to you so openly, you can tell me everything too. Is that not enough? Is it worth losing that, simply because we want more? That's the last thing I want. I told you last night that I can have violent mood swings . . . but this shouldn't drive you to the wrong conclusion . . . On the main points, I shall never change . . . So tell me. Will you be my friend?'

I was reeling after all this . . . The last thing I wanted was to pass some kind of final verdict, and I sensed that anything I said would be off the mark. I had just one desire: to stay close to her, no matter what the cost . . . nothing else mattered . . . I was not accustomed to ever asking a person for more than they were willing to give. Nevertheless, my heart felt strangely heavy. Fixing my gaze on her dark, clouded and imploring eyes, I prepared my words: 'Maria, I understand you perfectly . . . I can see why in the past you found yourself obliged to offer such explanations and I am happy with the idea that you are doing this so as not jeopardize our future relationship. This means that for you our friendship is precious . . .'

She nodded in approval. I went on: 'There may be no need for you to say any of this. But how can you know? We have only just met. It's better to be careful . . . I don't have as much experience as you. I am limited in my acquaintance and have always lived alone. Now I see that we have ended up at the same place but on different roads: we are both looking for someone, someone we can call our own . . . How wonderful it would be if we

could find that in each other . . . That is the most important
thing, everything else comes after that . . . As for what you said
about relationships between men and women, you can be sure
that I am nothing like the kind of person you fear. Truth is, I
have had no adventures, but I have never thought that I could
love someone unless I felt in her the same respect and strength
I find in myself. You just mentioned being degraded. In my
opinion, any man who allows that to happen is denying his
own person, and indeed degrading himself. I, too, love the natural world; in fact, I might even say that the more I stay away
from people, the closer I feel to nature. My country is one of
the most beautiful places in the world. Reading our history, we
learn of all the civilizations that rose and fell in those lands.
Lying under olive trees that go back ten or fifteen centuries, I
think about the people who collected their fruits through the
ages. On mountains studded with pine trees – slopes that seem
untouched by man – I would come across marble bridges and
carved columns. These are my childhood memories. These are
what fed my dreams. Nature's logic holds a higher place in my
estimation than anything else. So let's forget all this and just
allow our friendship to take its natural course. Let's not try
to set it on the false path or tie it up with decisions made in
advance.'

Maria tapped my hand with her index finger. 'You are not as
much of a child as I thought,' she said. With apprehensive eyes,
she looked me over. Her plump lower lip was pushed out more
than usual, making her look like a girl who was about to cry.
But her eyes were thoughtful and probing. It amazed me to see
how fast and dramatically her expression could change.

'You can teach me all sorts of things about your life and your
country, not to mention those olive trees,' she began. 'And I
can tell you a few things about my childhood and what I can
remember about my father. I don't suppose we'll have any

trouble finding things to talk about . . . but there's such an echo in here. It must be because there are so few customers . . . and that poor band over there . . . they're hoping the noise they make will impress their boss, if no one else. Oh, if only you knew what bosses are like in places like this!'

'Are they very rude?'

'Oh yes, very much so. You get to see men close up in these places. Our boss at the Atlantic, for instance. He is a very courteous man. Not just with customers – but with women with whom he is not doing business . . . There is no doubt that if I wasn't working in his cabaret he would flirt with me like a baron, until I was swooning over his fine manners. But if money is involved, he becomes a different man, and I suppose he would call this a "work ethic". It would be better to call it an "earning ethic". Because with us his rudeness borders on cruelty, even impropriety. It stems more from a fear of being cheated than any desire to preserve the seriousness of his establishment. Most probably, he is a good father and an honest citizen, but if you could see how he tries to sell us – not just our voices and our smiles and our bodies, but our humanity – your skin would crawl . . .'

This struck a distant chord. 'What did your father do?' I asked.

'Didn't I tell you? He was a lawyer. Why do you ask? Are you wondering how I ended up like this?'

I said nothing.

'It seems you still don't know Germany very well. There is nothing unusual about my situation. The money Father left us put me through school. We weren't that badly off. I was a nurse during the war. Then I continued at the academy. What savings we had left vanished with inflation. I had to earn money. I'm not complaining about that. There's nothing wrong with working. So long as it isn't demeaning. What bothered me was having no choice but to work with people who were always drunk and hungry for meat. They'd give such looks . . . I wouldn't just call it animalistic . . . because that in itself would still be natural . . . this was something beneath that . . . a bestiality fed by cruelty, hypocrisy and deceit . . . disgusting . . .'

She looked around the room. The orchestra was playing even louder than before. A woman dressed in a traditional Bavarian outfit and with hair like corn tassels was belting out a cheerful mountain folk song as she twirled about.

'Come on, let's go and sit somewhere quiet . . . it's still early,' Maria said. Then, looking at me intently, she added: 'Or am I boring you? I've been dragging you around all day now and talking your ears off. It's not good for a woman to be that friendly . . . I'm serious. I'll let you go if you're bored.'

I took her hands. I paused before answering.

I wasn't looking her in the face. Nevertheless there came a point when I was sure that she understood how I was feeling and I said: 'I'm so grateful to you.'

'I feel the same way,' she said, and she pulled away her hands.

As we stepped out onto the street, she said: 'Come on, we can go to a café not far from here. It's a wonderful place. Full of mad souls.'

'Romanisches Café?'

'Yes, do you know it? Have you been there?'

'No, I've only ever heard about it.'

She smiled. 'From friends who run out of money at the end of the month?'

I smiled and looked away.

The café was normally frequented by artists, but after eleven o'clock it would fill up with rich women hunting younger men, and I'd heard that this was when gigolos of all different ages would come and seek their fortunes.

It was early, so the place was still filled with young artists.

They were sitting in small groups, locked in heated discussions. Passing through the colonnades, we went up to the second floor, where we were only just able to find a free table.

Around us were young painters imitating the French with their long hair and pipes and their broad-brimmed black hats, and long-nailed writers leafing through their pages.

A tall blond young man with sideburns down to his lips waved from across the room and came over to our table.

'My greetings to the Madonna in a Fur Coat!' he cried. Taking Maria's face in his hands, he kissed her on the forehead and then the cheeks.

I cast my eyes down and waited while they chatted about this and that. I gathered that they had work in the same exhibition. Then, after giving Maria a vigorous handshake, he turned to me and, with what he must have thought to be a bohemian flourish, said: 'Adieu, my young sir.' With that, he left.

My eyes were still downcast when she said: 'What are you thinking?'

'Do you realize you just used the informal "you"?'

'Yes, I did. Do you mind?'

'What kind of question is that? Thank you.'

'Oof! You are always thanking me for everything.'

'In the East we are polite in that way . . . Do you know what I was thinking? How that man just kissed you and I wasn't even jealous.'

'Really?'

'And I'm curious to know why I wasn't.'

We looked at each other for a while. We searched each other's eyes, but this time with trust.

'Tell me a little about yourself,' she said.

I nodded to let her know I would. Earlier in the day I'd stored up so many things to tell her. But now I couldn't remember a single one. My mind was spinning with new thoughts. Finally,

I just started talking. In no particular order, I told her about my childhood and my years of military service, and the books I had read and the dreams I had held dear. I told her about Fahriye, the girl next door, and all the bandits I'd met after the war. I shared with her things I had until now shared with no one, or even admitted to myself. I was unburdening my very soul. This being the first time I had ever tried to explain myself, I wanted to be utterly candid, hiding nothing. But in my zeal to tell the whole truth, I put too much emphasis on my short-comings, thereby distorting it.

The floodgates had opened. My memories and emotions, suppressed for so long, came rushing through. When I saw how intently she was listening and reading my face for what I couldn't put into words, I opened up even more. Sometimes she would nod approvingly. At other times, she was open-mouthed with surprise. When I became overly agitated, she caressed my hand. When there was a note of reproach in my voice, she smiled at me with compassion.

At one point I stopped talking, as if propelled by some unknown force. I looked at my watch. It was nearly eleven. The tables around us were empty. I leapt from my seat. 'You're going to be late for work!' I cried.

She gathered up her things. Squeezing my hands more tightly than before, she rose from her chair. 'You're right,' she said. As she adjusted her beret, she added: 'What a beautiful conversation we've had!'

I walked her to the Atlantic. We hardly spoke along the way. We were both lost in thought, as we tried to understand what to make of our evening. As we approached our destination, a shiver ran through me.

'Because of me, you weren't able to go home for your fur coat. You'll catch a cold.'

'Because of you? That's true . . . because of you . . . but I am the one to blame . . . At any rate, it doesn't matter . . . let's just walk faster.'

'Shall I wait for you and walk you home?'

'No, no . . . no need for that . . . We'll meet tomorrow.'

'As you like.'

Maybe she was snuggling closer to me because she was cold. Outside the door that once again spelled Atlantic in electric bulbs, she stopped and held out her hand. It was as if she were wrestling with an idea. Then she pulled me over to the wall. Though she brought her face close to mine, she kept her eyes fixed on the pavement, and in a rushed whisper she asked: 'So you're not jealous of me then? Do you really like me that much?'

Now she looked up to gaze curiously into my eyes. I felt my chest tighten and my throat go dry, for no words could express my feelings. I was afraid that every word, indeed, every sound I uttered, might cloud those feelings and rob me of this bliss. Now there was a little fear in her expression. As I sank into despair, tears welled in my eyes. That's when her expression relaxed a little. She closed her eyes for a moment, as if to listen more closely. Then, taking my head in her hands, she kissed me on the mouth for the first time. A moment later, she had turned away to slip through the door of the club.

I rushed back to the *pension*. I needed time to think, to reflect on all that had passed. My precious memories of the night just gone were in need of a sanctuary, far from the noise of everyday recollection. In the same way that I had, only moments earlier, not dared say a word, lest it tear my sublime joy asunder, I now feared that the rough and tumble of my imagination would destroy the harmony I still felt inside me.

The *pension*'s dark stairwell now seemed quite charming and the corridor's stale air almost sweet.

From then on, I met Maria Puder every day. Together we wandered about the city. We almost never ran out of things to say to one another after that first night. If we talked about the people and vistas we saw along the way, it was because they offered us a chance to expand on our ideas and determine what we had in common. This intimacy came from thinking alike; in truth, it came from accepting one side of an idea while preparing to pay the price demanded by the other. But isn't this how souls come together, by holding another's every idea to be true and making it their own?

Mostly we visited galleries and museums. She offered instruction on the old masters and contemporary art, and we had heated discussions about their value. We returned to the botanical gardens several times and twice we went to the opera in the evening. But it was difficult for her to leave such a place by half past ten, so we stopped going. Then one day she said: 'It's not just a matter of bad timing, but there are other reasons I don't want to go to the opera. Singing in the Atlantic after leaving such a place feels so absurd, and so vulgar.'

I now spent only my mornings at the factory. I hardly ever saw the others in the *pension*. Occasionally Frau Heppner would latch onto me, saying: 'You seem to have let someone snap you up!' I would just smile, and leave it at that. I was particularly keen to keep Frau van Tiedemann from finding out. Maria would have seen nothing wrong in it, but I suppose that, being from Turkey, I felt the need for discretion.

Yet there was really nothing for us to hide. Since that first evening, our friendship remained within the agreed boundaries, with neither of us ever referring to that interlude in front of the Atlantic. In the beginning it was curiosity that kept us talking. We were always looking for new things in each other. Over time, curiosity gave way to habit. If, for whatever reason, we couldn't see each other for a few days, we'd begin to miss each other. When at last we met, we would walk down the streets hand in hand, as happy as children who'd been kept apart too long. How I loved her! I had opened my heart to the world I saw in her. Clearly she liked me too, and wanted to be with me. But she never allowed our relationship to progress. One day, when we were strolling through the Grunewald Forest on the outskirts of Berlin, she threw her arm around my neck and leaned against me, her hand dangling over my shoulder. She was drawing little circles in the air with her finger. On a whim I grabbed her hand and I kissed her palm. Straight away she pulled away, softly but with clear intent. Nothing was said. We carried on walking. But the message was clear enough to stop me from ever losing control of myself like that again. Sometimes we would talk about love. It was strangely dispiriting to hear how easily she could examine it from a distance. Yes, I had agreed to all of her conditions, and accepted them all. Nevertheless, I sometimes contrived to bring the discussion back to us. On these occasions we would analyse our friendship. In my opinion, love was not an absolute category. There were many kinds of love, just as there were many ways in which people could show their affection for one another. The name and the shape changed to fit the circumstances. In denying the love between a man and a woman its true name, we were deceiving ourselves.

Whereupon Maria wagged her finger and laughed: 'Oh no, my friend, no,' she said. 'Love is nothing like the simple compassion you describe, and neither is it a passion that comes and goes. It is something altogether different, something that defies analysis. And we are never to know where it comes from, or where it goes on the day it disappears. Whereas friendship is constant and built on understanding. We can see where it started and know why it falls apart. But love gives no reasons. So think about it. There are many people in this world that we like. I, for example, have several dear friends. (I might say that the esteemed gentleman comes top of the list.) Now am I in love with all of these people?'

I continued to press my point: 'Yes,' I said. 'You are a little in love with all those people you care for.'

Maria's answer was not what I was expecting. 'So then why did you tell me that you weren't jealous?'

Unsure of what to say, I thought for a time before saying: 'If a person truly has the ability to love, then he can never monopolize his beloved. And neither can his beloved monopolize him. The more he spreads his love, the more he adores his one and only true love. When love spreads, it does not diminish.'

'I thought Easterners thought differently about these things.'

'That's how I think about it.'

For a time, she stared into the distance, lost in thought, before saying: 'For me, love is something else entirely. It's beyond all logic and impossible to describe or define. It's one thing to like someone. To be consumed, body and soul, by desire is quite another. That's what love is to me – desire that's all-consuming. Desire that's impossible to resist!'

Speaking more confidently now – as if I'd caught her out – I said: 'What you're talking about is the moment. The moment that the love already inside you comes, through mysterious forces, to concentrate its full force on a single point. Just as warm sunlight can, by passing through a lens, turn to fire, so too can love. It's wrong to see it as something that swoops in from outside. It's because it arises from the feelings we carry inside us that it strikes us with such violence, at the moment we least expect.'

This particular discussion ended there, but we returned to the subject later. I'd come to the idea that neither of us was 100 per cent right. Hard as we might try to be open with one another, it was clear that we were driven by a host of other thoughts and desires that we did not begin to understand. While we agreed on a great deal, there were things about which we disagreed, and where we could agree to disagree, in deference to a larger goal. We were not afraid to reveal to each other the most secret corners of our souls and then quarrel. All the same, there were areas we left untouched, if only because we had no idea what they were. But I sensed their importance.

Having never known such intimacy before, I was desperate to protect it. And perhaps what I desired most was to possess her wholly and absolutely, body and soul, but I was so fearful of losing what I already had that I did not dare look away from it. I was, in effect, watching the most beautiful bird in all creation and keeping perfectly still for fear of frightening it away with a sudden movement.

But a dark thought still haunted me – that this stillness might, in the end, be more damaging than fearful hesitation. That it might stall what was alive between us, until it was as cold as stone: with every step not taken, we would be taking one step further apart from each other. Though these fears burned in silence, they troubled me more with every day.

But to behave differently I would have had to be another person. I knew I was going around in circles, but I had no idea how I might get to the heart of the matter, for I did not know what or where it was. I was no longer shy, no longer retiring. No longer did I shun company. I was willing, perhaps to an extreme, to be my true self, for all to see: but always on condition that I left the heart of the matter untouched.

I am not sure how capable I was then of thinking about all this with any clarity or depth. It's only now that I can go back to that time and see myself as I was twelve years ago and come to these conclusions. Time has likewise allowed me to think again about Maria.

I knew then that she was prey to a host of conflicting moods. Some days she was listless, even cold. Some days she would be bursting with energy, showing me such fervent interest as to take my breath away, and even provoking me. But then it would pass, and we would go back to being friends. Like me, she could see that we had arrived at an impasse and that we might be stuck there for ever. But though she did not find in me what she desired, there were things in me she cherished enough to refrain from doing anything that might push me away.

Fearful of what might happen, lest these warring emotions came out into the light, we kept them hidden deep inside our hearts. Thus we went back to being two dear friends – always seeking each other out, always looking for new ways to please each other, and always the richer for it.

Then suddenly everything changed, setting us on an entirely new course. It was towards the end of December. For Christmas her mother went to the outskirts of Prague to visit distant relatives. Maria was pleased.

'Nothing in the world tries my patience more than those pine trees decked out in candles and stars,' she said. 'It's not because I'm a Jew. Considering that I find these meaningless rituals utterly ridiculous, and the people who find joy in them even more so, it goes without saying that I don't have any time for Judaism either, or its strange and unnecessary rules and rituals. In any case, my pure-blooded German mother is a Protestant. She's only attached to these rituals because she's old. If she calls me an atheist these days, it's not because she gives any great importance to the rules of religion, but because she's worried I might rob her of her final years of peace.'

'Don't you find anything special about New Year?' I asked.

'No,' she said. 'How is it different from any other day? Was it distinguished by nature for any particular reason? And how important is it to mark the passing of another year? That's not nature's work either – it's a human fabrication. The road we embark on the day we are born is the road we travel until the day we die, and however we choose to divide it up, it's pure artifice. But let's leave philosophy to one side and go some-where for New Year's, if that's what you want . . . My work at the Atlantic finishes before midnight, to make room for all their special attractions. So we can go out together and get drunk like everybody else . . . It's good to go wild every once in a while and get lost in the crowd . . . What do you say? After all, we've never danced together.'

'No, never.'

'I actually don't really enjoy dancing, but sometimes the person I'm dancing with does and so I find a way to bear it.'

'I'm not sure I'll like it.'

'Neither am I . . . but never mind, friendship is all about making sacrifices.'

On New Year's Eve we had dinner together, lingering at the table until it was time for her to go to work; when we got to the Atlantic she went backstage to change, whereupon I took myself over to my old table. The hall was festooned with streamers, tinsel and gaudy lanterns. Most of the customers looked as if they were already drunk. They were traipsing across the dance floor, kissing and groping. It all left me feeling strangely depressed.

'So what's all the fuss,' I thought to myself. 'Really, what was so special about this night in particular? We make things up to suit what we need to believe. It would be better if everyone just went home and got into bed. What are we supposed to do? Hug each other and go home like all the rest? With one big differ-ence: we aren't going to kiss . . . I wonder if I can even remember how to dance?'

During my months at the Academy of Fine Arts in Istanbul,

a few of my friends had taken dance lessons from the White Russians who were everywhere in the city at that time, and from them I'd learned a few steps. Indeed, I'd come close to mastering a certain kind of waltz . . . But how could I be sure of pulling that off tonight, after more than a year and a half? 'You fool,' I said to myself. 'You'll never make it through an entire dance.'

Maria's act ended sooner than I expected, and then all hell broke loose. Each customer had a different idea of what they wanted to see next. As soon as Maria had changed, we moved on to a large establishment called the Europa, opposite the Anhalter train station. This was a far cry from the small and intimate Atlantic. As far as the eye could see, there were hundreds of couples swirling around a massive dance floor. The tables were covered with bottles of all colours. Some people were already asleep, heads lolling or resting in another's lap.

Maria seemed strangely agitated. Punching me in the arm, she said: 'If I'd known that you were just going to sit here and mope, I would have asked another young man to escort me.'

I was astonished to see how quickly she knocked back the glasses of the deliciously dry Rhein wine that they kept bringing to our table. She insisted that I do the same.

It was after midnight that the place went truly wild. The air rang with shouts and laughter as the band belted out one old waltz after another, and the dancers swept across the floor. Here it was, in all its starkness: the frenetic jubilation of a country no longer at war. And how they saddened me, these emaciated creatures with their protruding cheekbones and glimmering eyes, which seemed to me to be possessed by a dreadful malady! These young men, giving themselves over to an unbounded exuberance. These young women, so convinced they were rebelling against society as they surrendered to sexual desire.

Putting yet another glass in my hand, Maria whispered: 'Raif, Raif. This won't do at all . . . Can't you see how hard I'm trying to avoid sinking into despair? Just let it go. Better to slip out of our skins for just one night. Imagine that we are no longer ourselves. We are two other people, lost in this great crowd. Take a good look around you – are any of these people really what they seem to be? Let me tell you what I won't stand for: being the odd ones out. Pretending to be the only ones with brains for fine feelings. Time to drink and be merry!'

She was, I could see, well on her way to being drunk. She'd been sitting across from me, but now Maria came around the table to sit beside me, draping an arm over my shoulder. My heart was pounding. I might have been a bird caught in lime. I noticed, too, that she thought I was upset. But nothing could be further from the truth. I was, if anything, taking my happiness too seriously: I was, one might say, too happy to smile.

They were playing another waltz. Leaning over, I whispered: 'Let's dance then. But I'm really not very good . . .'

Pretending she hadn't heard the second half of my sentence she leapt up at once: 'Let's dance!'

We went twirling through the crowd. This was nothing like dancing; we could do no more than sway with the bodies pressing in on us from all sides. But neither of us complained. Maria had her eyes fixed on me. Now and again something glimmered in her dark and absent eyes, something I couldn't understand, and this, along with the faint but intoxicating scent of her warm body, threw me off guard. I could not help but believe that it meant something to her, to be this close.

'Maria,' I whispered, 'how can one person make another person so happy? What amazing powers we must have, hidden deep inside us.'

Once again, I saw that light flicker in her eyes. But then, after a long stare, she bit her lip. Her eyes now looked empty and fogged: 'Come on, let's sit down. What a crowd! They're starting to get to me.'

Back at the table, she downed one glass of wine after the other. Then she got up, saying: 'I'll be right back.' And she staggered off.

I waited some time for her. Despite all of my protests I had ended up drinking too much. But I didn't feel drunk so much as dazed. My head was throbbing. A quarter of an hour had passed but still she'd not come back. I started to worry. I got up and went to the washrooms, thinking that perhaps she had fallen somewhere. Women were freshening up their make-up in front of mirrors or trying to pin up parts of their dresses that had come loose. I couldn't find Maria anywhere. I looked at all the women in the corners of the room and the ones who had curled up and fallen asleep on the sofas. I couldn't see her anywhere. Seized by a great anguish, I ran from one room to the next, knocking into tables, pushing my way through the crowds. Leaping down three steps at a time, I made it to the ground floor and looked for her there. Still no sign of her.

Then I caught sight of her through the misty glass of the revolving front doors. There she was, an effigy in white. Rushing outside, I let out a cry. For here was Maria Puder, leaning against a tree, cradling her head in her hands, face pressed into the bark. She was wearing nothing but a thin woollen dress. Heavy snowflakes were falling on her hair and the back of her neck. When she heard my voice, she turned and smiled and asked: 'Where have you been?'

'Where have *you* been?' I cried. 'What are you doing? Have you lost your senses?'

Bringing her finger to her lips, she said: 'Shush. I came out to get some air and cool off. Come on, let's go.'

Straight away I pushed her back inside and sat her down on

a stool; then I went upstairs to pay the bill and get my coat and her fur coat from the cloakroom. With that we headed off, our feet pressing deep into the snow.

Clinging to my arm, she struggled to keep pace. There were drunken couples here and there along the side streets. In the avenues there were milling crowds – scantily clad women, laughing and singing as if they had decided, two or three hours after midnight, to set off on a springtime jaunt.

Maria was pulling me along faster and faster through this drunken crowd. To those who called out to her, or attempted an embrace, she offered a cursory smile, skilfully extracting herself to pull me along. While I, for my part, realized how wrong I'd been, to think she was too drunk to stand on her own two feet.

After a time, we came to streets that were quieter, and we slowed down. But she had still not caught her breath. Letting out a deep sigh, she turned to me and said: 'So? Are you happy with how things went tonight? Did you have a good time? Oh, I had a wonderful time, such a wonderful, wonderful time . . .'

Her smile gave way to a giggle, and then a coughing fit. Soon her chest was rattling as if she were about to choke, but still she was clinging to my arm. When she had recovered herself, I said: 'What's all this, then? Didn't I warn you? You've caught a chill.'

She replied with a broad smile: 'Oh, but I had so much fun!'

Now it was me, fearing she might cry. I wanted to get her home and tucked into bed as soon as possible.

As we neared her building, she began to sway. It seemed as if she had lost her strength, and with it her will. But the cold air had revived me. I was holding her by the waist now and trying not to step on her feet. Crossing one street, we nearly tumbled into the snow. Now she was murmuring something I could not quite hear. At first I thought she was humming a song, but when I realized she was speaking to me I pricked up my ears: 'Yes . . . so that's the way I am,' she said. 'Raif . . . oh dear Raif . . . that's just the way I am . . . Haven't I told you? One day I'm like this and the other like that . . . but there is no need to be sad about it. You are such a good boy . . . I have no doubt about that.'

At this point, she succumbed to hiccups, but soon she was mumbling again: 'No, no, there is no need to be sad about it . . .'

Half an hour later, we were at her front door. Leaning back against the stairwell wall, she waited.

'Where are your keys?' I asked.

'Don't be angry with me, Raif . . . don't be angry . . . Here! Right in my pocket!'

Stuffing her hand into the pocket of her fur coat, she pulled out a key ring, on which I could see three keys.

I opened the door. When I turned to help her up the stairs, she shot past me to race up the stairs.

'Be careful!' I shouted.

Breathless, she replied: 'No. I can go up by myself.'

As I had her keys I went up after her. After going up a few floors, I heard her calling to me through the darkness: 'I'm here . . . open this door.'

Groping for the door, I opened it. Together we stepped inside. She switched on the lights. The furnishings were old but relatively well preserved. And there, on the side, was a beautiful oak bed.

I was standing in the middle of the room. Tossing off her fur coat, she gestured at a chair: 'Sit down.'

Perching on the edge of the bed, she kicked off her shoes and her stockings. In no time at all, she had pulled her dress over her head, thrown it on a chair and slipped under the quilt.

Rising to my feet, I wordlessly held out my hand. She let her eyes pass over me, as if seeing me for the first time, as a drunken smile spread across her face. I lowered my eyes. When I next looked up, she was sitting up and staring at me, open-eyed and curious, blinking now and again as if she had just woken up. The white coverlet had slipped, to reveal her right arm and shoulder. They were as pale as her face. She had her left elbow propped up on the pillow.

'You'll get cold.'

Tugging at my arm, she sat me down on the bed. Then she snuggled up to me, opening my hands, so that she could rest her face in them.

'Oh, Raif. So you can be like this, too? You have every right . . . But what can I do? If only you knew . . . if only . . . But we had such a wonderful time, didn't we? Oh, didn't we ever . . . No, no, I know that! Don't pull your hands away . . . I have never seen you like this. How wonderfully serious you can be! But why?'

I looked up. She was kneeling next to me on the bed now, cupping my face with her hands: 'Look at me,' she said. 'It's not what you think . . . I can prove it to you . . . I can prove myself to you . . . Why are you just sitting there? You still don't believe me? You don't trust me?'

She closed her eyes. She seemed to be struggling to capture an elusive thought. Her brows were furrowed, her forehead creased. When I saw those bare shoulders trembling, I pulled up the quilt and held it there, to keep it from slipping down again.

She opened her eyes. She smiled in surprise. 'So that's the way it is . . . You're smiling too, aren't you?' Unable to say any-more, she gazed off into a corner.

Her hair had fallen down over her face. The light illumin-ating one side of her face also lit up her eyelashes, casting a shadow over the bridge of her nose. Her lower lip was trembling ever so slightly. In that moment she was more beautiful than her painting, more beautiful than the Madonna of the Harpies. With the arm holding the quilt, I pulled her closer.

I felt her body shaking. Her breathing was shallow.

'Of course . . . of course,' she said. 'Of course I love you. And so much . . . Could it be any other way? I must love you . . . I certainly do. But why are you so surprised? Did you think it could be any other way? I know how much you love me . . . and there is no doubt that I love you just as much . . .'

She pulled me towards her, to cover my face with fiery kisses.

I woke up the next morning to deep and measured breathing. Her head was resting on her arm. Her back was turned. Her hair fanned out over the white pillow. Her lips were slightly parted, and above them was the finest down, which rose and fell with every trembling breath she took.

Falling back onto the pillow, I looked up at the ceiling and waited. I was full of impatience. I longed to know how she would look at me when she woke up and what she would say, but for whatever reason I feared that same moment. From the moment I'd opened my eyes, my peace of mind had gone. And I had absolutely no idea why. Why was I trembling like a convict awaiting a verdict? What more could I ask from her? What more did I expect? Hadn't I been granted all my heart desired?

How empty my heart felt now! But also, how heavy! Something was missing, but what? I felt bereft, like a man who stops on the street, remembering that he has forgotten something at home, but cannot for the life of him remember what it is, and after rummaging through his mind and his pocket, finally gives up, and continues reluctantly on his way, while the doubt still gnaws at him.

Some time later, I noticed that I could no longer hear Maria's rhythmic breathing. Lifting my head, I stole a glance. She was staring into the distance. She hadn't moved at all; her hair was still falling over her face. Though she knew I was watching her, she continued to stare unblinking at that fixed but unknown point in the distance. She must have been awake for some time, I realized, as an invisible clamp tightened around my chest and the fear in my heart grew.

The more I dwelt on my absurd anxieties and needless, groundless apprehensions, the more I castigated myself for letting my paranoia and wretched intuition darken what should have been the brightest days of my life, and the more I despaired.

'Are you awake?' she asked, without turning her head.

'Yes . . . Have you been awake for long?'

'I just woke up.'

I took courage from her voice, which had, for so long now, been the sweetest sound I knew. I welcomed it like an old friend. Just to hear it was to be suffused in happy memory. But the peace it brought me was short-lived. She had used the formal 'you', whereas we had recently begun to shift back and forth between formal and informal. What was I to make of her use of the formal 'you' on the morning after this night we had just shared?

Perhaps it was because she was only half awake.

She turned around to face me. She was smiling. But this was not the warm, sincere smile I'd come to know so well. It was more the sort of smile she flashed at customers at the Atlantic.

'Are you getting up?' she asked.

'Yes, I am!' I said. 'And you?'

'I'm not sure . . . I don't feel terribly well. I'm feeling a bit fragile . . . probably from all that drink . . . My back is hurting too . . .'

'Chances are you caught a chill last night! What did you

think you were doing, going outside like that, with almost nothing on?'

She shrugged and turned away.

I got up, washed my face and quickly got dressed. I could feel her eyes on me.

There was tension in the room. I felt the need to make light of it: 'We've both run out of things to say, you and I . . . what's happening to us? Have we already grown bored with each other, like an old married couple?'

She looked up with uncomprehending eyes. This made me even more upset, so I said no more. But then I went over to the bed: I wanted to caress her, shatter the wall of ice between us before it had a chance to grow. Whereupon she sat up, to let her legs swing down off the bed, draping a thin cardigan over her shoulders. And, all the while, studying my face. Something was bothering her, and holding her back. Finally, she began to speak. In a very calm voice, she asked: 'Why are you upset?'

And then, for the first time, I saw her pale face go pink. Her chest heaving, she continued: 'What more do you want? Can there be anything more you could want? . . . But let me tell you. I do want more than this, much more, and yet it's still beyond my grasp. I've tried everything, but to no avail. From now on, you can be happy. But what about me?'

Her head fell to her chest. Her arms dangled lifelessly at her sides. Her toes were just touching the rug. Her big toe was turned up and the others were curled downwards.

I pulled up a chair to sit across from her. I took her hands in mine. My voice was trembling, as befits a man who is about to lose his most precious belonging and the very meaning of his life.

'Maria,' I said, 'Maria. My Madonna in a Fur Coat. What's happened all of a sudden? What have I done to you? I promised that I would ask nothing of you. Haven't I kept my promise? Why you are saying this, at a time when we should be closer to each other than ever.'

Shaking her head, she said: 'No, my friend, no! We are further from each other than ever before. Because I have lost all hope. This is the end . . . I told myself that I would only experience this once. I thought maybe only this was missing. But no . . . I still feel the same emptiness inside . . . only it's greater . . . What can be done? It's not your fault. I'm just not in love with you. But I know only too well what this world of ours requires: that after decreeing that I fall in love with you, I must, having failed to fall in love with you, nevertheless abandon all hope and never love another, ever again . . . But it is not in my control. So that is just the way I am. I have no choice but to accept the way things are . . . Oh, how I wish . . . how I wish it were otherwise . . . Raif . . . my good-hearted friend . . . please believe that I wish as much as you – and perhaps even more than you – that it were otherwise. What can I do? Right now I don't feel anything but the sour taste of the drink in my mouth and an ache in my back that is getting steadily worse.'

She was quiet for a while. She shut her eyes, and her lovely face softened. In a voice so sweet she might have been telling a fairy tale from childhood, she said: 'Last night, especially after we came here – oh, the things I hoped for . . . I dreamed of a magic wand that would change me utterly, give me a new heart, one that combined the innocence of a little girl with the power to embrace all creation, so that when I woke up in the morning I would wake up to a new world. But the truth is another country . . . the skies here are cloudy . . . my room is cold . . . I feel so estranged from everything around me. Despite the intimacy between us, you are still so far away, another person in another body . . . my muscles are so tired and my head aches . . .'

She fell back onto the bed and lay down on her back. She put her hands over her eyes and went on: 'So I suppose this means that people can only get so close to each other and then they must drift apart, each time they try to take one step closer. I can't tell you how much I did not want our intimacy to have a limit, or an end. What truly saddens me is seeing how empty my hopes have turned out to be . . . Now there is no point in deceiving one another . . . we can no longer speak openly as we did before. We sacrificed it all and for what, why? Nothing at all! In attempting to possess something that was never there we lost something we already had . . . Is it all over? I don't think so. I know that neither of us are children. But we do need to spend some time away from each other, some time to rest. Until we feel the overwhelming desire to see each other again. Enough, enough! Raif, I shall call you when that time comes. Perhaps we will be friends again and all the wiser for it. We won't expect so much from each other, or think that we can give so much . . . But now it's time for you to go . . . I really do need to be alone . . .'

She drew her hand away from her eyes. Looking at me, almost pleadingly, she held out her hand. I took the tips of her fingers and said, 'Adieu.'

'No, no, not like that . . . You are angry with me . . . What have I done to you?' she cried.

Mustering all my strength to remain calm, I said: 'I am not angry, only sad.'

'Can't you see that I am too? Can't you see? Let's not part like this. Come here.'

Placing my head on her chest, she caressed my hair. She placed her cheek on mine.

'Smile once for me and then go,' she said.

I smiled and then hurried out of the room, my face hidden in my hands.

Out on the street I began walking aimlessly. There was no one outside and most of the shops were still closed. I was heading north. Trams and omnibuses with steamed-up windows passed me by. I walked . . . along the cobblestone pavement and past houses with darkened façades . . . I kept walking . . . I opened my jacket because I was sweating. I came to the end of the city. And I kept walking . . . I walked under the railway bridges and over the frozen canals . . . still walking. Always walking. I walked for hours. Without thinking. My eyes blinking away the cold, I picked up my pace, until I was almost running. On either side of me were well-kept pine forests. Now and then a clump of snow tumbled off a branch. Cyclists passed me by, and in the distance I heard a train shaking the ground. I walked . . . then on my right I saw a good-sized lake full of skaters. Turning into the woods, I walked towards it. Among the trees were long, criss-crossed tracks left by skis. In a grove protected by a wire fence, little snow-covered pine saplings trembled like children in white capes. In the distance I made out a two-storey wooden country inn. Turning to the lake, I watched girls in short skirts and young men with clipped trousers skating side by side. They would lift up one foot to spin around, before speeding off hand in hand, to disappear behind a headland. The girls' coloured scarves fluttered in the wind and so too did the boys' blond hair, as together they swayed first to one side and then to the other, and with every step they seemed to change in height, rising and falling as one.

And I was all eyes, all ears. Sinking ankle-deep into the snow, I trudged towards the lake, taking in every detail. Passing behind the country inn, I headed for the trees across the lake. I remembered having been here before, but I could not remember when, nor could I figure out exactly where I was. A few hundred metres behind the lodge were a few old trees on a hill. I stopped. Again I gazed out at the skaters on the ice.

By now I'd been walking for about four hours. I had no idea why I'd turned off the road or why I'd not yet turned back. The burning in my head had subsided; the tingling in the base of my nose was gone. All I could feel was a terrible hollowness in my heart. A door had opened, promising the sublime, but then it had slammed shut, robbing my life of all hope and meaning. I felt as bereft as if I'd awoken from the sweetest of dreams to face the pain of truth. In no way did I hold this against her, I felt no anger. I was only sad. All I could think was: 'It shouldn't have come to this.' The truth was she could not find it in her to love me. And with good reason. Never in my life had anyone loved me, ever. In any case, women were mysterious creatures. Passing my mind over all the women I had known or observed, I was driven to conclude that true love was beyond them. When they were in a position to love, they did not. Instead they ached for the unattainable – the opportunities missed, the salve that their broken hearts longed for – thereby mistaking their yearnings for love. But soon I realized that I was judging Maria unfairly. In spite of everything, I knew full well that she was nothing like those others. And I had seen how much she was suffering. It was not possible for her to suffer like that purely out of pity for me. She was suffering because she longed for something she could not find. But what was it? What was I lacking? Or rather, what were *we* lacking?

How painful it is, after thinking that a woman has given us everything, to see that in truth she has given us nothing – to see that instead of having drawn her closer, she is further away than ever!

It should never have come to this. But as Maria had said, there was nothing to be done; on my part especially . . .

What right did she have to treat me like that? I could have carried on as I was, shunning human company and leading a mediocre existence, but at no point having to face how very empty my life was: I'd have dragged on through life, convinced that my strange temperament allowed me no more, and never would I have known what it meant to lead a happy life. I'd have suffered from loneliness, while still believing that one day I might be rescued. Such was my state of mind when Maria, or rather her painting, came into my life. She had swept me away from my dark and silent world, delivering me to the land of truth and light. And now she had vanished, offering no reasons, and as suddenly as she'd come. But for me there was no hope of sinking back into my old torpor. For as long as I lived, I would travel far and wide, meeting with people whose languages I did or did not know, and everywhere I went, I would be looking for Maria Puder. In every pair of eyes, I would be searching for the Madonna in a Fur Coat. I knew from the outset that I would never find her. Yet it was not in my power to give up searching. She had condemned me to a lifelong quest for a cypher, for someone that did not exist. She should never have done this to me.

The years ahead seemed too bleak to endure. And neither could I find a reason to bear such a burden. As I battled with these thoughts, a curtain lifted. I remembered where I was. This lake before me was the Wannsee. One day, while I was travelling with Maria Puder to Potsdam to see the park of Frederick II's New Palace, she'd pointed it out to me through the train window, telling me that more than a century earlier, the great poet Heinrich von Kleist and his beloved had committed suicide under the trees where I was now standing.

What had brought me here? What had possessed me to return to a place I'd only glimpsed in passing? It was almost as if I'd come straight here, in answer to a promise. Could it be that, after parting with the one person I trusted most in this world – after hearing her declare that there was a point beyond which two people could not be together – I'd come to this spot where two people had gone together, even into death, as some sort of retort? Or was I merely seeking to convince myself that there were lovers in this world who refused to pull away from each other? I cannot say. My recollection of my train of thought is hazy. But all of the sudden the ground beneath my feet seemed to be on fire! I could almost see the two lovers stretched out before me, one bullet in her breast and one in his head. And there, twisting through the grass, were two streams of blood, flowing from their wounds and running into the puddle that was forming around my feet. Their blood, like their fate, was conjoined. And there they still were, just a few steps away. Side by side . . . Turning on my heels, I raced back along the same path that had brought me.

From below I could hear laughter rising from the lake. I could see couples spinning around, their arms round each other's waists, as if setting out on an endless journey. Now and again, the inn's front doors flew open, letting out snatches of music and stomping feet, as those who had skated long enough climbed up the hill, most probably to drink grog and enjoy a bit of dancing.

They were having fun. They were alive. While I stood apart, locked up inside my own head, and watched – not, as I now understood, from above, but from below. It was not a surfeit of idiosyncrasy that had led me to shun society. I had pulled away because there was a part of me missing. But life was meant to be lived, as these people were doing. They were taking their share of life, and giving something back. What was I in comparison? What did my soul ever do, apart from gnawing away at me like a woodworm? This gramophone, this wooden inn, this ice-covered lake, these snow-covered trees and this jumbled crowd: they were all busy with the tasks that life had given them. There was meaning in everything they did, even if I could not see at first glance. And I was but the wheel that had spun off its axle, still searching for reasons as I wobbled off into the void. No doubt I was the most useless man in the world. The world would be no worse off without me. I expected nothing of anyone and no one expected anything of me.

From that moment, something in me changed, setting my life on a new course. From then on, I have believed myself to be useless and worthless. I have, on occasion, felt myself on the verge of coming back to life – of returning to the land of the living. As I mulled over my change in circumstances, I would, for a few days, allow myself to be consoled. But then I would return to my deep-rooted conviction that this world had no use for me. There was nothing I could do to free myself from its influence – so much so that even today, so many years later, I can still recall the full force of that moment when I pulled away from the world, my courage shattered. I can see just as clearly that I was not mistaken in my conviction . . .

I raced down to the asphalt road and headed back to Berlin. I hadn't eaten anything since the previous night, but I did not feel hungry so much as nauseous. My legs weren't tired, but every muscle in my body was taut. I was walking slowly now, steeped in thought. The closer I came to the city, the greater my despair. I simply could not accept the fact that I would be spending all my days without her – the very idea seemed remote, impossible, absurd . . . yet I could never go to her with my head bowed, to beg. It was not in my nature; it would serve no purpose . . . I conjured up mad scenes that had more than a little in common with my childhood fantasies, except that they were even bloodier and more improbable. How splendid it would be to call her to the telephone just before she was to take the stage at the Atlantic and (after I had asked her forgiveness for having disturbed her and bade her farewell) pump a bullet into my head, while she listened at the other end! Upon hearing this deadly sound, she would pause, uncomprehending, before madly screaming 'Raif! Raif!' into the receiver. And if, by chance, I happened to hear her cries as I lay there on the ground, taking my last breath, I would die smiling. With no idea of my whereabouts, she would flail about in desperation, too distracted to call the police, and when, the next day, as she leafed through the papers with trembling hands, reading the details of this mysterious tragedy, she would seize up with remorse and regret, knowing she would never be able to forget me, now that I had bound myself to her memory in blood.

By now I was close to the city, passing over and under the same bridges. It was almost evening. I had no idea where I was going. I went into a little park and sat down. My eyes were burning. Leaning back, I looked up at the sky. The snow was turning my feet to ice. But I sat there for hours, nevertheless. A strange numbness spread through me. Oh, to die here of cold, to be buried without fanfare the next day! What would Maria do, when she chanced upon the news a few days hence? What sort of shadow would pass across her face? What regret would overtake her?

My thoughts kept going back to her. I got up and continued on my way. I still had hours to go before I reached the city centre. I began to mumble to myself as I walked. Everything I said, I said to her. My head was spinning with a thousand brilliant ideas, a thousand seductive illusions – just as it had been during our first few days together. But I knew, nevertheless, that no words existed that could change her mind. As my eyes filled up with tears, I would tell her in a trembling voice that it was nigh impossible for two people to find the kind of intimacy that we had already shared, therefore unthinkable for us to part for such an absurd reason . . . At first it would seem strange to her, to see a man as meek and calm as I speaking with such passion, but the moment would arrive when she reached out slowly to take my hands and smile and say: 'You're right!'

Yes . . . I had to see her and explain everything. I had to persuade her to reverse this frightful decision to which I had agreed so easily this morning. And she *would* reverse it. It occurred to me now that she might even have been offended by the speed with which I'd left the house, without a word of protest. I had to see her at once, before the night was out.

I wandered aimlessly until eleven in the evening, when I began to pace up and down in front of the Atlantic, waiting for her to arrive. But she didn't. Finally I asked the doorman with the sequined coat: 'I don't know, she didn't come tonight,' he said. Her illness must have taken a turn for the worse, I now decided. I raced over to her building. Her window was dark. She must have been sleeping. Thinking it best not to disturb her, I went back to the *pension*.

For three days I waited for her outside the Atlantic, going afterwards to her front door to look up at her dark window, and never once did I find the courage to do more than head back to my room. Every day I sat there, trying to read. I was only turning the pages, oblivious to the words, and sometimes I would gather my resolve and go back to the beginning, but after reading the first few lines my mind would be wandering once again. I knew that there was nothing more for me to do save accept her decision as final and wait for time to pass. But in the evenings my feverish imagination took hold, tormenting me with impossible thoughts. And then, late at night, I would rush out onto the street, in contravention of all my daytime resolutions, to wander around her house and any other street I thought she might take. By then I was too ashamed to ask the doorman with the sequined coat, so I made do with watching the entrance from a distance. Five days passed like this. I saw her every night in my dreams, closer to me than she ever was before.

On the fifth day, after seeing that she had still not turned up for work, I telephoned the Atlantic and asked to speak to Maria Puder. They told me that she had not been in for a few days on account of illness. So she really was seriously ill. Did I have any reason to doubt that? Why had I needed some sort of confirmation? She was hardly going to change her working hours or tell the doorman to drive me away! I set out for her building, determined to wake her up even if she was asleep. Whatever limits she set on our relationship, I surely had the right to do so. Yes, we'd both been very drunk. But it wasn't right to attach such importance to the morning after.

Breathlessly, I raced up the stairwell and without a moment's hesitation pressed the doorbell. Just one short ring. Then I waited. Not a sound from inside. I pressed again, several times, this time for longer. I was hoping for footsteps but I heard nothing. Then the opposite door cracked open: it was a maid, who looked half asleep.

'What do you want?' she asked.

'I'm looking for the person who lives here.'

After giving me a good look, she growled: 'There's no one there.' And my heart skipped a beat.

'Did they move?'

When she spoke again, her voice was softer, perhaps because she'd heard the panic in my voice: 'No, her mother never came back from Prague. And she fell ill. No one to look after her so the doctor at the infirmary sent her off to hospital.'

Hearing this I rushed across the landing. 'Where is she then? Is it serious? Which hospital did they take her to? When . . .'

Taken aback by my frantic questions, the maid retreated a step: 'Stop shouting. You'll wake up everyone in the building . . . They took her away two days ago. I think it was Charité Hospital.'

'What's wrong with her?'

'I don't know.'

I didn't even think to thank her. I left her staring in amazement as I flew down the stairwell four steps at a time. The first police officer I came upon told me where I could find Charité Hospital. I went straight there, with no idea of what I was going to do. On first glimpsing the enormous stone building from a hundred metres away, a chill went through me. But I walked resolutely, passing the large gate and calling for the porter to come out of his room to speak to me. Though I was given a level of courtesy beyond what I deserved – I had, after all, arrived in the middle of the night and forced him out into the freezing cold – the porter could tell me nothing about Maria. He had no news of a woman having been admitted recently, let alone what she might be suffering from or where I might find her. Although he tried to cover up his frustration with a smile, he had the same reply for every question: 'If you can come tomorrow morning at nine, they'll be able to tell you.' That was all he would say.

It was during that long night, as I paced the hospital's high stone walls, that I came to appreciate just how much I loved Maria Puder and how desperately I was attached to her; I thought about nothing but her. When I looked up to see patients peering down at me, through windows bathed in a pale yellow light, I tried to guess which one hers might be, and oh, how I longed to be at her side, wiping the sweat from her brow and attending to her every need!

That night I came to understand how it was possible to be more attached to another person than to life itself. And that night I also came to understand how hollow life would be without her. As hollow as a walnut shell, tossed by the winds.

As the wind hurled the snow from one wall to next, it came close to blinding me. The streets were deserted. Now and again a white car went through the front gate, and a little later it came out again. A police officer gave me a long stare when passing me for the second time. Passing me for the third time, he asked me why I was there. I told him I knew someone inside and he suggested that I should go home and rest and come back in the morning, but when we ran into each other after that, he gave me a pitying glance and moved on.

As the sky brightened, the streets slowly came to life. Now there were more white cars going in and out of the hospital gate. At nine o'clock sharp, I got permission from the doctor on duty to come inside, even though it was not a visiting day. It was my desolate expression, I imagine, that convinced him to make an exception for me.

Maria Puder was in a single room. I was shown in by a nurse who told me that I should not stay long as the patient needed rest. She was suffering from pleurisy, but the doctor did not think her condition was serious. Maria turned her head, and the moment she saw me, she smiled. But then her expression changed. She looked alarmed. Once the nurse had left us alone, she said: 'What's wrong, Raif?'

Her voice was still the same. But her pale face had taken on a yellowish hue. Coming closer to her, I said: 'What's happened? Have you seen yourself?'

'It's nothing . . . I suppose it will pass . . . but *you* look exhausted.'

'Last night the people at the Atlantic told me you were ill. I went to see you at home and the maid across the hall told me they had brought you here. They didn't let me in, so I waited until it was morning.'

'Where?'

'Here . . . outside the hospital.'

She looked me up and down, with the gravest of expressions. She seemed about to say something, but then she stopped.

The nurse came into the room. I bade Maria goodbye. She nodded, but she did not smile.

Maria Puder stayed in hospital for twenty-five days. They might have kept her there longer, but she told the doctors that she was growing restless and that she could look after herself better at home. Carrying with her a great deal of advice and a long list of prescriptions, she left the hospital one snowy day and made her way home. I have little recollection of what I did over those twenty-five days. I don't think I did anything but visit her in the hospital, to sit at her bedside, watching her vacant stare, her face drenched in sweat, and her chest rising and falling as she struggled to breathe. Indeed, I was not really living; because if I had been, I would remember a few details, if nothing else. All I can recall is an overwhelming sense of dread. I was terrified I might lose her. Whenever her fingers strayed beyond the covers, or her feet quivered beneath it, I saw the shadow of death. I could see it even in her face, her lips, her smile: I sensed in them a surrender, an acceptance of some awful fact, a readiness even – as if all they needed now was to find the right opportunity. And what would I do then? Yes, I would have to take care of the final stages, preserving the peace, choosing a cemetery as I consoled her mother, who would have returned from Prague by then, and finally with a few others we would lay her to rest in the earth . . . After a while everyone would leave, but I would return in secret to stand alone beside her grave. And that was when it would begin. That was when I would truly lose her for ever. And then what would I do? I could imagine it in detail up to that moment, but what would happen afterwards? Yes, after we had laid her to rest in the earth and all the others had gone their separate ways, what was I to do? From then on there would be nothing more for me to do for her. And there would be nothing more absurd or meaningless than to still be here on earth. It was soul-destroying, just to contemplate. One day, when she'd begun to show some sign of improvement, she said: 'Speak to the doctors. Have them let me go.' And then, in the most casual of whispers, she added: 'You'll do a better job of looking after me.'

Without further ado, I raced out of the room. The consultant wanted her to stay a few more days. So we came to an agreement. And then, at last, on the twenty-fifth day, I draped her fur coat around her shoulders and led her down the stairs. I took her home in a taxi and the driver helped me take her up; but even so, by the time she'd undressed and got into bed, she was exhausted.

From then on I was truly the only one who looked after her, except for the old woman who came in the morning to do the cleaning, light the large tiled stove and cook a meal for the patient. Despite my pleas, she refused to summon her mother. In the letters she wrote to her with trembling hands, she said: 'I'm fine. You have a good time and spend the winter there.'

'She wouldn't be any help to me if she came. She's the one who needs help . . . she would worry needlessly, and before long I would be worrying too.' And then, in that same blithe whisper, she would add: 'And you're already looking after me. Or are you tired and beginning to lose patience with me?'

But she wasn't joking when she said these words, and she wasn't smiling. Since falling ill, she'd almost never smiled. When she first set eyes on me in the hospital, she'd smiled, but after that she'd turned serious. Whenever she asked me for something, or thanked me for something, or spoke of anything at length, her manner was solemnly pensive. I'd sit with her until late at night, returning early in the morning. Later on I took to sleeping on a good-sized sofa in the same room, using the blanket from her mother's bedroom. We'd not said a word about our contretemps – although it would not be right to call it that – our little chat on the first morning of the New Year. My visits to her in the hospital, and our life together since I'd brought her home – it had all happened so naturally there'd seemed no need to discuss it. Indeed, we both avoided even the slightest reference to the new arrangements. Yet clearly she was mulling something over. As I pottered about the apartment, or read to her out loud, I could feel her eyes on me constantly. It was as if she were looking for something in me. One evening I was sitting in the lamplight, reading her a long story by Jakob Wassermann entitled 'The Mouth That Was Never Kissed'. It was about a teacher who'd never known love, and who'd grown old without so much as admitting to himself that he longed for the human warmth of love. It was a masterful depiction of a man struggling to keep his dying hopes alive, unbeknown to anyone around him. After the story finished, Maria closed her eyes and fell into silence. Then she turned to me and in a languid voice asked: 'You've never told me what you did after New Year's Day, during that time we weren't seeing each other.'

'Nothing,' I replied.

'Really?'

'I don't know . . .'

Another silence fell over the room. It was the first time she'd broached this subject. But I was not surprised. Indeed, I realized that I had been waiting for this very question for some time. But instead of answering, I gave her something to eat. Then I wrapped her up nicely and sitting beside her I said: 'Shall I read you something?'

'As you wish.'

I had become accustomed to reading her something faintly tedious after supper to help her fall asleep. I hesitated for a moment.

'Why don't I tell you about the first five days of the new year. That will put you to sleep right away,' I said.

She did not smile at my little joke; she just nodded, as if to say, 'Go ahead then.' I began very slowly, pausing now and then to gather up my memories. I told her where I'd gone after leaving her house, and what I'd seen and what thoughts had passed through my mind as I'd walked around the Wannsee and how, as evening fell, I'd headed back to Berlin – to circle her building; and finally I told her about the last evening when I'd heard she'd been taken into hospital – how I'd raced straight over and waited there until morning. My voice was calm, as calm as if I were recounting events that had happened to someone else. I poured it all out – everything I could remember, piece by piece – lingering on the details, stopping from time to time to attempt an explanation. She listened in silence, her eyes closed. She was so still I thought she might be sleeping. Nevertheless I went on. It was almost like speaking to myself. I admitted to feelings I had never acknowledged until now, and I questioned them, but before I could draw any meaningful conclusion, I would move on. Only once, when I was telling her about how I had imagined bidding her goodbye on the telephone, did she open her eyes. She looked at me intently, and then shut her eyes again. Every line of her face was still.

I concealed nothing, I felt no need to do so. Because I had no particular motive. My imaginings seemed so strange to me now, so distant in time, and so far away. That is why there was not a trace of subterfuge or calculation in what I said about her, or about me: in that regard, I was merciless. I could not recall a single one of the delusions that had assaulted me during that night I'd spent waiting outside, nor did I seek them. I wished only to tell a story and nothing more. I judged each event on its own merits, and not by what it meant to me personally. And she gave me her full attention, though she never stirred.

I felt this in my bones. When I told her of my thoughts as I sat at her bedside, and of how I'd imagined her dying, she blinked several times . . . but nothing more . . .

At last I reached the end of my tale. I had nothing more to say, and neither, it seemed, did she. We sat there in silence for perhaps ten minutes. Then she turned to face me, opening her eyes and, for the first time in a long while, she smiled faintly (or so it seemed to me) and in a soft voice, she said: 'Shall we go to bed?'

I got up and prepared my bed, then I undressed and switched off the lights; but I couldn't get to sleep. I could tell from her breathing that she was still awake too. With time, I could feel my eyelids growing heavy, but still I waited for that soft and steady whir I had come to know so well. I struggled not to drift into sleep. Yet I was still the first one to succumb.

Early in the morning I opened my eyes. The room was still dark. A faint light filtered through the curtains. But that soft and steady whir that I had come to know so well – I could not hear it. An eerie silence filled the room. For we had both reached our limit. There was so much – too much – welling up in our hearts. I could feel that, almost viscerally. And at the same time I was gripped by a fearsome anxiety: how long had she been awake? Or had she not even gone to sleep? Neither of us was moving, as our thoughts swirled around the room.

Slowly I looked up and, as my eyes adjusted to the darkness, I realized that Maria was looking at me with her head propped up against a pillow. 'Good morning,' I said. I went into the other room to wash my face. When I came back I found the patient in the same position. I opened the curtains. I put away the night lamp. I gathered up my bedding and tidied the sofa. I opened the door for the maid when she arrived and I helped Maria drink her milk.

I did all this with hardly a word. I tended to these tasks every morning, before heading off to the factory, where I would stay until noon. In the afternoon I would read to her from a book or a newspaper. I'd tell her about everything I'd seen and heard until it was evening. Wasn't this the way it had to be? In truth, I wasn't sure. But everything had fallen into place in a way that felt natural. No desires plagued me. I thought of neither the future nor the past; I lived only in the present. My soul was like a glassy, windless sea.

After I had shaved and dressed, I told Maria that I was leaving.

'Where are you going?' she asked.

Surprised, I said, 'You know. I'm off to the factory.'

'What if you didn't go today?'

'That's possible, but why?'

'I don't know . . . I want you to be with me all day.'

I took this to be an invalid's whim, but I said nothing. I opened the paper the maid had left on the side of the bed.

Maria seemed agitated, almost distressed. I put down the paper and sat down beside her and placed my hand on her forehead. 'How are you feeling today?'

'I'm fine . . . much better . . .'

Despite her stillness, I could sense she wanted me to keep my hand on her forehead. And as I kept it there, I could almost feel her gathering up all her will.

Trying to sound light-hearted, I said: 'So you're doing well! So then, why didn't you sleep at all last night?'

That threw her for a moment. Blood rushed up from her neck into her cheeks. I could see that she was looking for a way not to answer. Then suddenly she shut her eyes, leaning back as if drained of all energy. In the softest of voices, she said: 'Ah, Raif . . .'

'What's wrong?'

She pulled herself up. 'It's nothing,' she gasped. 'I just don't want you to leave me today . . . Do you know why? I suppose it has to do with what you told me last night. I know that once you've gone, it will all come racing back and I won't have a moment's peace . . .'

'If I'd known that, I'd never have told you,' I said.

She shook her head: 'No, that's not what I mean . . . I'm not thinking about myself . . . It's just that now I can't trust you anymore! I'm afraid to leave you alone . . . You're right, I hardly slept at all last night. I couldn't stop thinking of you. I could only think of everything you did after you left me that day and how you wandered around outside the hospital, and all those other things you told me about and even the things you didn't . . . that's why I can't leave you alone anymore! I'm afraid . . . and I'm not just talking about today . . . I shall never let you out of my sight, ever!'

Little beads of sweat had formed on her brow. Gently I wiped them away. My palms felt warm and wet. I gazed at her in awe. She was smiling, the first pure and innocent open smile I had seen in some time; but tears were streaming down her cheeks. Taking her head in my hands, I pulled her into my arms. Now her smile was even softer, much, much softer; but the tears kept falling. She didn't make a sound, and her chest was still. I had never imagined that anyone could cry in such stillness. Her hands were like two little white birds resting on the white bedcover and I took them in mine to caress them. Her fingers curled, opened again and then tightened into a fist in the palm of my hand. The lines on her palms were as thin as the veins of a leaf.

Slowly, I let her fall back onto the pillow.

'Don't strain yourself,' I said.

Eyes glimmering, she said: 'No, no,' and she held onto my arm. Then as if she was speaking to herself, she said: 'Now I know what's been missing. It's not anything in you, it's in me . . . I cannot believe . . . I simply could not believe that you loved me that much and so I assumed I wasn't in love with you ... Now I understand. It seems that people have taken from me the ability to believe ... but now I can ... you've taught me how ... I love you ... not madly, but I love you with a clear mind ... I want you ... such an overwhelming desire ... if only I can get better ... When will I get better?'

Without answering, I dried the tears in her eyes with my cheeks.

Then I stayed at her side until she felt strong enough to stand up. If I had to step out to buy food and fruit or stop off at the *pension* to get a change of clothes, she was alone for two or three hours, which seemed to me like a terribly long stretch of time. When I took her by the arm and sat her down on the couch, or placed a thin sweater over her shoulders, I felt that boundless happiness that comes from devoting your life to another. We sat in front of the window, gazing outside for hours, saying nothing, only occasionally looking at each other to smile; her illness had brought out the child in her and my happiness had done the same for me. In a few weeks she regained much of her strength. When the weather improved, we began to venture out onto the streets, to stroll for half an hour.

She would take great care getting dressed; when leaning over, she would often be overtaken by a fit of coughing, so I even had to put on her stockings for her. Then she would put on her fur coat and I would gently lead her down the stairs. Fifty metres from the house, we would sit down on a bench to rest. From there we would amble across the Tiergarten, to the shores of a pond, to watch the swans glide over the weedy waters.

Then one day it all came to an end ... It was that simple, it ended so abruptly that I failed to grasp the enormity of what had happened ... I was only a little surprised, but deeply saddened; and I would never have thought that such an event would leave such a great and lasting effect on me.

In those final days I was reluctant to go back to the *pension*. Though I had continued to pay for my room in advance, the manageress had become cold with me because I was so seldom there. One day, Frau Heppner said: 'If you have moved elsewhere, then let me know and we can inform the police. Otherwise they will hold us accountable.'

I tried to make light of the situation: 'How could I possibly leave you?' I said and then went up to my room. I had lived there for over a year and now the personal effects I had brought with me from Turkey, like the books strewn across the room, seemed utterly foreign to me. Opening my suitcases, I pulled out a few necessities and wrapped them up in newspaper. Then a maid came into the room.

'There's a telegram for you, it's been here for three days now,' she said and handed me a folded piece of paper.

At first I could not take in what she was saying. Somehow, I could not bring myself to take the telegram from her hand. No, this piece of paper could have nothing to do with me . . . I hoped against hope that, whatever tragedy was looming, I could fend it off for as long as I refused to read that telegram.

The maid stared at me in disbelief. Deciding that I was not about to move, she put the telegram on the table and left the room. Whereupon I seized the telegram and tore it open.

It was from my brother-in-law. 'Your father has died. Have wired money. Come at once.' Nothing more. Only nine or ten words, the meaning all too clear . . . yet I stood there looking down at the page. Reading it over and over, each and every word. Then I stood up, stuffed my newly packed parcel under my arm and went out.

What had happened? I could see that nothing around me had changed. It was all just as it was when I came. I could see no change in me, or in the world around me. Most likely Maria was waiting for me at the window. Yet I was not the same

person I had been half an hour earlier. Thousands of kilometres away, a man had stopped breathing; and though this
had happened days, if not weeks, ago, neither Maria nor I had
noticed. Each day had been the same as the one before. Yet
suddenly a trifling piece of paper had turned our world upside
down, swept it out from under my feet, pulling me away from
this place and reminding me of the distant land whence it had
come, the land that was now reclaiming me.

I could see it so clearly now. How mistaken I had been, to
assume my life of the past few months was real; and to hope it
would last for ever! But still, how desperately I wished to fend
off the inevitable! It shouldn't have been like this. It should not
have mattered so much where we were born, whose child we
were. All that mattered was that two people had found each
other and achieved a rare happiness. The rest was incidental. It
had no choice but to fall into place, giving way to that great
felicity.

But I knew in my heart that this was not how events would
unfold. For our lives were governed by trivial details. Indeed,
trivial details were what true life was made of. The logic in our
minds had always been at odds with the logic of life itself. A
woman is gazing out of a train window when a fleck of coal
dust lands in her eye; without giving the matter a moment's
thought, she rubs it in. A gesture as slight as this can end in a
beautiful eye losing its power to see. Or a brick comes loose in
the wind and crashes down on the head of an illustrious man.
And what good would it do, to ask which is more important –
an eye or a fleck of coal, a brick or a brain? We have no choice
but to accept such accidents for what they are, along with all
the others that life thrusts upon us.

Could this really be true, though? Yes, the world was governed by forces beyond our grasp or understanding. That much
was true. But even if they were modelled on the natural world,

there were certain absurd forms of corruption that could be avoided. What, for instance, was binding me to Havran? A few olive groves, two soap factories and a family I barely knew and had no interest in getting to know better . . . My life was here in Berlin. I was bound to this place in every way imaginable. So then, why could I not stay? The answer was simple: our businesses in Havran would come to a halt, my brothers-in-law would stop sending me money, and I would be left floundering. There was also the question of my passport, my residence permit and the embassy register – matters whose importance we all too often underestimate, though in my case they were of huge significance, shaping my life's very direction.

When I explained all this to Maria Puder, she said nothing for a time. Then she gave me a strange smile, as if to say, 'Didn't I tell you?' While I, for my part, struggled to maintain my poise, fearing that I might look ridiculous if I opened my heart to her. Yet several times I said: 'What should I do?'

'What should you do? Well, you should go of course . . . I'll go away for a while as well. In any case I won't be going back to work any time soon. I can stay with my mother outside Prague. I suppose life in the countryside will be good for my health. I can spend the spring there.'

It felt odd, to be putting my dilemma to one side to discuss her plans in such a way. Now and then she threw me furtive glances.

'When are you going?' she said.

'I don't know. I should probably leave as soon as the money arrives . . .'

'Maybe I'll leave before you do . . .'

'Really!?'

She laughed at my surprise. 'You have always been a child at heart, Raif. Only a child would be this agitated in the face of the inevitable. And anyway, we have plenty of time, so we can talk things through before we decide anything . . .'

I went out to see to a few trifling matters that I needed to deal with before leaving Berlin, and to give notice at the *pension*. I was not a little surprised when I got home in the evening and found Maria all packed and ready to leave.

'What is the point in wasting any time?' she said. 'I'll set out straight away and leave you free to take care of everything before your journey. And then . . . oh, I don't know . . . the long and the short of it is that I've decided to leave Berlin before you do . . . I don't really know why . . .'

'As you wish.'

We said nothing more about it. We had planned to think it over and then decide, but as it turned out we did not say a single word.

She left the following evening by train. We stayed at home all afternoon. Together we sat gazing out of the window. We took note of each other's addresses. We agreed that with each letter I wrote, I would send her an envelope with my address on it, to be sure her letters reached me. She did not, after all, know how to write in Arabic script, nor did our postman in Havran know how to read the Latin alphabet.

For an hour, we indulged in idle, aimless conversation: how long the winter was lasting this year, how there was still snow on the ground in late February. It was all too clear that she wanted the time to pass quickly, while I clung to the absurd hope that we could stay sitting side by side for ever more.

Nevertheless it surprised me, how we clung to the mundane. Now and then we would exchange puzzled smiles. When it was finally time to leave for the station, we seemed almost relieved. From that point on time flew by with terrifying swiftness. She was adamant that I should not stay with her in the train compartment after we had stowed away her luggage, and that we wait together on the platform instead. There we spent another twenty minutes exchanging foolish smiles, but for me it seemed no longer than a second. A thousand thoughts were racing through my mind. There was no way to do them justice in such a short space of time, so I did not even try. But I'd had a whole day to speak my heart. So why this lukewarm farewell?

Only in the final minutes did Maria Puder seem to lose her composure. This reassured me. I suppose it would have saddened me greatly to see her go without showing any emotion at all. She kept taking my hand then letting it go: 'It's ridiculous, isn't it?' she kept saying. 'Why do you need to go anyway?'

'But you are the one leaving. I'm still here,' I said.

She seemed not to hear me. She took my arm. 'Raif . . . I'm going now.'

'Yes . . . I know.'

It was time for the train to depart. A conductor shut the wagon door. Maria Puder leapt up onto the step, but then she leaned back towards me. Speaking very slowly, but lingering on every word she said: 'I am leaving. But I will come whenever you call for me . . .'

At first I did not understand what she meant. She paused then added: 'I will go anywhere!'

Now I understood. I wanted to take her hands and kiss them. But Maria was already inside and the train was chugging forward. Seeing her at the window, I hurried over, then stopped. I slowed down. Waving her goodbye, I cried: 'I shall call for you . . . Have no doubt! I shall!'

She nodded with a smile. I could tell from her expression that she believed me.

I felt the sadness of a conversation left unfinished. Why had not we broached the subject yesterday? Even when we were

144

stowing away her bags, we were still talking about the winter and then the joys of travelling. Why had we avoided all mention of the matters most dear to us? But perhaps it was better this way. What would come of all those words? Would we not have come to the same conclusion? Maria had found the best way . . . of that I was certain . . . an offer and an affirmation . . . brief, spontaneous and indisputable! There could not have been a sweeter parting. All those passionate words I'd kept hidden inside me – how bland they seemed to me now, and how feeble . . .

I was beginning to understand why she had left before me. She would have found Berlin most irksome, had I left first. Certainly I did, even as I rushed around blindly seeing to tickets and itineraries, visas and passports. How strange I felt, every time I happened onto a street down which we had walked together! Even though there was nothing to be sad about. Once I had been back in Turkey long enough to arrange my affairs, I would send for her. As simple as that . . . I gave my daydreams free rein. I could already see the beautiful villa I would build for us just outside Havran, and the hills and forests we would visit together.

Four days later I returned to Turkey, passing through Poland and Romania. There is nothing of note to say about that journey and my subsequent years in Turkey . . . Only after I had boarded the ship in Constanţa did I begin to reflect on the events that pulled me back to Turkey. The truth finally sank in: my father had died. It shamed me deeply to know it had taken me this long. There was, in fact, no reason for me to feel any genuine affection for him; he had always been a stranger to me. Had someone asked me if my father had been a good man, I would have been at a loss for words. For I had never been close enough to know how good or bad he was. It was hard even to think of him as a real person: for me he had always been an abstract idea. A father. A bald man with a round grey beard who came home every evening in frowning silence. Who saw no reason why he should pay the slightest attention to his children, or to our mother. How different he was from the fathers I saw in the Havuzlu coffee house, drinking *ayran* as they laughed and cursed over their backgammon boards ... How much I would have liked to have had a father like that ... If ever he saw me in the company of such fathers, he would glower and shout: 'What are you doing here? Go over to that stove and get yourself a hot sherbet. Then go straight back to our neighbourhood and play there!'

Even when I was older and back from the army, he treated me the same. The more I grew in my own eyes, the smaller I was in his. If I happened to share my thoughts with him, he would look away in contempt. If in later years he indulged me in my whims and did not deign to argue with me, it was further proof of his low opinion.

There was, nevertheless, nothing in my mind that could sully his memory. What I felt most keenly was not his empty presence, but his absence. The closer I came to Havran, the greater my sadness became. It was difficult to imagine our home or our town without him.

There is no need for me to go on about this. Indeed, I would rather not speak of the ten years that followed, but I should still allow for at least a few pages about this, the emptiest chapter of my life, if only to clarify certain matters. I did not return to a warm welcome. My brothers-in-law treated me with derision, my sisters treated me like a stranger, and my mother was more miserable than ever. The house was empty, my mother having moved in with my eldest uncle. As I was not offered a place there, I found myself living alone in our enormous house with an elderly family retainer. When I looked into taking over my father's business, I was informed that his estate had been divided up before his death. And I could not get a clear answer from my brothers-in-law about what had been left to me. There was no talk of the two soap factories; but over time I learned that one had been sold by my father some time ago and the other by my brothers-in-law. No doubt this was because my father had run through all the money and gold that he had generally been thought to be hoarding. My mother knew none of this. When I asked, she said: 'How would I know, my son? We can only conclude that your late father left this world without telling us where he buried it. Your brothers-in-law never left his side in his final days . . . Did he know that he was dying? No doubt in his last breath he told them where he had buried everything . . . What should we do now? We could at least speak to the treasure finder . . . they know everything.'

And the truth was that my mother visited every treasure finder in or near Havran. Following their advice, we dug around the bases of nearly every olive tree and wall in the area. What little money she had left, she spent on this enterprise. My sisters went out with the treasure finders too, but they were reluctant to spend any of their own money; and I noticed that my brothers-in-law found our endless excavations quite hilarious.

The harvest season had come and gone, so there was no income from the olive groves. I managed to procure a small sum by selling some of their future crops in advance. My goal was to get through the summer, and then, with the arrival of the olive season in the autumn, to do everything in my power to set matters straight, after which I would send for Maria Puder at once.

We wrote to each other frequently after my return to Turkey. Those hours I spent reading or responding to her letters offered me some relief from the tedious problems that defined my life during the muddy spring and suffocating summer that followed. I had been home for a month when Maria returned to Berlin with her mother. I sent my letters to the post office in Potsdam Square and she picked them up there. In the middle of the summer I received an odd letter from her. She told me that she had some very good news for me, but that she would only be able to tell me in person when she came to Turkey. (By then I'd told her that I'd be in a position to send for her in the autumn.) And though I asked, in each subsequent letter, what her good news might be, she never told me. She just said it would have to wait until she joined me.

So, yes, I waited – not just until the autumn. I waited for ten long years . . . only then did those glad tidings reach me . . . by which I mean, only last night . . . but let me leave that for now. Let me tell the story as it unfolded.

I spent that summer with my boots on, riding on horseback over hills and mountains, inspecting my olive groves. How shocking it was to know that my father had left me the driest, most inhospitable and inaccessible plots of land. Whereas the olive groves on the fertile plains near our town – where every tree provided more than half a sack of olives – he'd left to my older sisters, or rather, my brothers-in-law. Most of my own olive trees had not been pruned or cleaned for years and had begun to grow wild, and soon enough it was clear to me that, in my father's time, no one had bothered to go up and harvest them.

Reflecting on my father's illness, my sisters' nervousness and my mother's anguish, I could only conclude that some mischief had gone on in my absence. Yet I kept hoping that by continuing to work as hard as I could, I would put my own affairs right, and every letter from Maria bolstered up my courage and optimism.

At the beginning of October, when the olives were ripening and I began to think it might be time to call for my beloved, the letters suddenly stopped. I'd fixed up the house by then, ordering new furniture from Istanbul, along with a bathtub, for which I'd retiled the old washroom, all much to the shock and disdain of the people of Havran and my family in particular.

I had not seen fit to disclose my reasons, so they dismissed me as some sort of fop, shallowly aping European fashions. Indeed, it was sheer madness for a man in my tenuous position to take the small sum he had scraped together from lenders and the olive harvest and spend it on mirrored bathroom cupboards. I bore their accusations with a bitter smile. They could not, after all, begin to understand why I was doing all this. And neither did I feel the slightest compulsion to offer an explanation.

But nearly twenty days had passed without a letter from Maria and I'd fallen prey to a terrible foreboding. Prone as I was to suspicion and paranoia, I imagined a thousand possible reasons for her silence. I kept writing to her – letter after letter. Receiving no answer I slipped into the deepest despair. Even before her letters had stopped altogether, they'd been coming less frequently. She'd been writing less and, it seemed, with more difficulty . . . I brought out all her letters and read them all again. In recent months, there'd been veiled, even evasive, passages that were utterly unlike what I had come to expect from a woman as open as she: it was almost as if she had something to hide, something for which she had not been prepared. So much so that I began to ask myself if she really wanted me to call for her, or if – dreading the prospect of having to break a promise – she feared that I might do so. By now I was reading whole volumes into each line, driven to distraction by every joke and unfinished thought.

My letters achieved nothing. My worst fears came true.

I did not hear from Maria Puder again. I did not even hear her name . . . until yesterday . . . But I am jumping ahead . . . A month later, my last letter to her came back with a stamp saying 'unclaimed, return to sender'. That was when I lost all hope. Even now it still shocks me, to remember how much I changed over the next few days. I could not move, or see, or feel, or think: what had given me strength to live had been swept away, leaving only my shadow.

Now I bore no resemblance whatsoever to the man I had been in the early days of the new year. I had thought myself bereft, but that was nothing in comparison to the desolation that had now overtaken me. For then I'd had a dream to cherish – the hope that we might return to intimacy, the determination to change her mind. But now I was utterly ravaged. The vast distance between us meant that there was nothing I could do. Shutting myself up at home, I wandered from one room to the next, reading her letters and the letters that had been returned to me, lingering over points I'd failed to note until now, and smiling bitterly.

I gave up on work, and on life in general. There was indeed nothing left for me. I stopped shaking the olive trees, stopped taking their fruit to the factory to be pressed into oil. Sometimes I would pull on my boots and head out into the countryside, where I could wander without fear of seeing another human face; returning late at night, I would stretch out on a divan for a few hours' sleep. Waking in the morning to a terrible ache in my heart, I would wonder why I was still alive.

And so it was that I slipped back into the life I'd led before meeting Maria Puder: my days were just as empty and aimless as before, but also more painful. Because there was a difference: I'd believed, in my ignorance, that there was nothing more to life than this. I was suffering now because I knew that there was another way to live. I no longer took any notice of my surroundings. The joys of life were for ever closed to me.

For a brief while, a woman had pulled me out of listless leth-argy; she had taught me that I was a man, or rather, a human being; she had shown me that the world was not as absurd as I had previously thought and that I had the capacity for joy. But from the moment we lost touch, I lost the benefit of her influ-ence. I went back to my old ways. Now I understood just how desperately I needed her. I was not the sort of man who could walk through life alone. I needed her at my side. I could not live without her support. Yet somehow I carried on living . . . as you can see . . . If this can be called living, then that is what I did . . .

I never heard from Maria again. I did write to the *pension*, but the manageress wrote back to inform me that Frau van Tiedemann was no longer in residence and had left no forward-ing address. Who else could I have asked? In one of her letters Maria had told me that she and her mother had moved house after returning from Prague. But I did not have the address. When I thought about how few people I'd come to know dur-ing my two years in Germany, I was truly shocked. I had never strayed far from Berlin, but I'd explored its every avenue and cul de sac. I'd been to every museum, gallery, botanical gar-den, forest, lake and zoo. Yet in a city of millions I had only spoken to a handful of people and only really come to know one.

Perhaps she'd been all I needed. I suppose that is what any of us need: one single person. But what if that person wasn't really there? What if it all turned out to be a dream, a chimera, a delu-sion? I had lost the power to hope, and with it the power to believe. My distrust of others was so great, and so bitter, that I sometimes scared even myself. Everyone I met, I met with hos-tility. Everyone I encountered, I assumed to be full of malice. This attitude did not soften with the passage of time: as year followed year, it became more pronounced. The mistrust I felt for people had turned into spite. I shunned people who tried to get close to me. I was most fearful of those I felt were closest to me, or who I feared might grow closer. 'Not after what she did to me . . .' I'd say to myself. But what had she done? I didn't know; and this was why my imagination dwelt on the gravest and most dreadful possibilities. That was just the way things were in this world . . . and what was the point of holding to a spontaneous promise made at the moment of parting? Far better to sever ties there and then, without dispute. My letters had waited, uncollected, at the post office . . . never to be answered . . . and now everything I'd believed in was gone. Who could say what new adventure had swept her off her feet? Who could know what greater and more intimate happiness she'd discovered in the arms of another? To leave all that, simply because she'd made a promise to win the heart of a naive boy, to follow him blindly into a life she knew nothing about . . . In the end, her good sense had prevailed.

Yet why, despite all my careful thought, was I unable to adjust to my new circumstances? Why did I recoil from any new opportunity that came my way? Why was it that when someone tried to get close to me, my first thought was that they might hurt me? There were occasions when I forgot myself and let someone come closer. But then I'd hear that doom-laden voice again, to set me straight: 'Don't forget, don't forget! Never forget that *she* was even closer . . . but even so, she left . . .' If ever anyone drew close enough to raise my hopes, I was quick to dampen them down: 'No, no, she was much, much closer . . . and now there is nothing between us at all . . . Yes, that's how things turned out!' To believe or not to believe . . . every day – every moment of the day – that was the question that terrorized me. No matter how hard I tried, I remained in its grip . . . I got married . . . Even on our wedding day, I knew that my wife was more distant from me than anyone else in the world. We had children . . . I loved them, always knowing that they would never restore to me what I'd lost . . .

I was never interested in any of the jobs I took. I worked like a machine, without knowing what I was doing. I allowed myself to be cheated and from this I took a strange sort of pleasure. My brothers-in-law made a fool of me and I did not mind. What property I had left went towards the wedding expenses and my debts. The olive groves were of little value. They were offered for even less to buyers wealthy enough to invest in derelict property. But there was not a single buyer willing to pay half a lira for a stump of a tree that only produced seven or eight liras' worth of a harvest per year. Only to save me from dire straits and to keep the family wealth intact, my brothers-in-law paid off my debts and bought my olive groves. I had nothing left but a house with fourteen rooms that was in a state of ruin and a few sticks of furniture. My wife's father was still alive and working as a civil servant in Balıkesir; with his help I was able to secure a position at a firm in the provincial capital. I stayed there for many years. As my family responsibilities grew, I became steadily more detached from the world; for I had utterly lost the will to connect. Then my father-in-law passed away and I was left with my wife's brothers and sisters. I was unable to support them all on my forty-lira wage. So a distant relative of my wife's arranged a job for me at a firm in Ankara, where I am still working today. Shy though I was, there was hope that I'd advance quickly in this firm, on account of knowing a foreign language. But nothing of the sort happened. No matter where I was, I failed to make my presence felt. Opportunities abounded. Many different people gave me a fleeting hope that I might start my life over, drawing on my heart's abundant reserves. But I just could not shake off my cynicism. There was only one person I'd ever believed in. I'd believed in her so deeply that – once deceived – I lost the will ever to believe in anyone again. I felt no anger towards her. I could not begrudge or resent her, or even think ill of her. Rather, I begrudged and resented everyone in the world; because for me she was the symbol of humanity. As the years rolled by and my bond to her persisted, I felt even more aggrieved. She must have long since forgotten about me. Who could say where she was living now, or with whom she spent her time? In the evenings, as I listened to my children's wailing and my in-laws' squabbles, and my wife's slippers as they padded across the kitchen, and the clatter of plates as she saw to the washing up, I'd close my eyes and imagine Maria Puder somewhere. Perhaps, at this moment, she was walking through the botanical gardens with a like-minded friend, admiring the trees' red leaves. Perhaps she and this like-minded friend were strolling through a sombre gallery, admiring the works of great masters, in the light of the setting sun. One evening I stopped off at the local shop to pick up a few things. As I was stepping outside, I heard the overture of Weber's *Oberon* playing on the radio of a young bachelor who lived across from us. I nearly dropped my shopping. This was one of the operas I'd seen with Maria. She'd been especially fond of Weber; when we were out strolling, she'd always whistle this same overture. I felt such a fresh longing for her at that moment that we might have parted only yesterday. The pain of losing something precious – be it earthly happiness or material wealth – can be forgotten over time. But our missed opportunities never leave us, and every time they come back to haunt us, we ache. Or perhaps what haunts us is that nagging thought that things might have turned out differently. Because without that thought, we would put it down to fate and accept it.

I never received much attention from my wife or my

children – or from anyone in my family, for that matter. But, equally, I never expected it. That cloak of worthlessness that had first settled over me on that strange New Year's Day in Berlin – it had now become my skin. What use was I to these people, beyond providing the loose change they needed to buy bread? What we crave from others far more than money or material assistance is love and attention. A family man who receives neither is not a family man at all: he is merely putting a roof over the heads of strangers. How I longed for the day when they no longer needed me, and all this would come to an end! Over time my life came to be defined by that faraway hope. I lived almost like a convict, dragging myself from day to day. If I also treasured each passing day, it was because it took me closer to the end. I lived like a plant, unconscious and uncomplaining and without a will. Emotion was beyond me. I felt neither sadness nor joy.

How could I feel anger towards people? The one I had deemed most precious, splendid and beloved had served me up the cruellest fate, so how could I expect anything else from the others? I could no longer love, or risk any form of intimacy, for I had been deceived by the one person I'd trusted and believed absolutely. After that, how could I trust anyone again?

When I thought about the future, I imagined years of tedium, until at last the longed for day arrived and it all ended. I wanted nothing more. Life had dealt me a bad hand. But there it was. Best not to blame myself or anyone else. Best to accept that this was how it was, and would needlessly continue to be, and find some way to endure. I found life tedious, but that was all. I had no other complaint.

Then one day . . . yesterday to be precise – Saturday – I came home and undressed. My wife told me that we needed a few things for the house: 'The shops are closed tomorrow, so you'll need to make one more trip to the market!' Reluctantly I got dressed. I walked as far as the fish market. It was a fairly hot day. There were plenty of people wandering the streets, waiting for the cool of evening to dispel the dust. I'd finished my shopping, and I was walking towards the statue with my packages under my arm. I decided to return home on the asphalt roads instead of the twisted back streets, even though it took a little longer. A giant clock hanging outside one of the shops read six o'clock. Suddenly someone took my arm.

A woman bellowed into my ear: 'Herr Raif!'

How shocking, to hear someone address me in German! I was seized by the urge to flee. But the woman had a tight grip on me.

'No, I am not mistaken. It is really you, Herr Raif! Good Lord!' she cried, as passers-by looked askance. 'Can a person really change that much?'

Slowly I raised my head. Though I didn't need to see her face. I knew who she was from her voice and her great bulk.

'Ah, Frau van Tiedemann, I never would have thought of seeing you here in Ankara,' I said.

'Not Frau van Tiedemann . . . it's Frau Döppke! I sacrificed a 'van' for a husband, but I'm doing nicely, nonetheless!'

'Congratulations . . . so . . .'

'Yes, yes, as you might imagine . . . not long after you returned to Turkey we left the *pension* . . . naturally together . . . we went to Prague . . .'

At the mention of Prague, a knife went through my heart. Impossible to suppress the thought. But how could I ask her? She knew nothing of my relationship with Maria. If I asked after her, what would the woman think? And then, wouldn't she ask me how I knew Maria? What would she say next? Wouldn't it be far better for her never to know? So many years had gone by – ten years, indeed, even a little more. What use would there be in her knowing the whole story?

Noticing that we were still standing in the middle of the street, I said: 'Come, let's sit down for a moment. We have so much to talk about ... I still haven't got over the shock of seeing you in Ankara.'

'Yes, it would be very nice to sit for a while, but our train is leaving in less than an hour ... We can't miss it ... I would certainly have called you if I'd known you were in Ankara. We arrived last night. And we are leaving tonight ...'

I had finally noticed a quiet little sallow-faced girl standing beside her. She was about eight or nine years old. I smiled: 'Is this your daughter?'

'No, a relative ... my son is finishing his law degree.'

'Are you still recommending him books to read?'

For a moment she seemed confused, but then she remembered and smiled: 'Yes, you're right, but he doesn't really pay any attention to what I recommend. He was still so young then ... twelve years old or so ... oh, dear God, how quickly the time flies!'

'Yes ... but you haven't changed at all!'

'And neither have you!'

Her earlier words had been more truthful, but I chose not to mention this.

We made our way down the hill. I had no idea how I was going to ask after Maria Puder and so I chattered needlessly about matters that had nothing to do with me.

'You still haven't told me why you've come to Ankara.'

'Ah yes, well, let me tell you all about it ... we are just passing through. Stopping over for the night.'

She agreed to sit for five minutes at a lemonade stand where she continued her story.

'My husband is currently in Baghdad ... As you know, he trades in the colonies.'

'But Baghdad is not a German colony!'

'Oh, I am aware of that, my dear . . . but my husband special-izes in food from the warmer climates. He's in Baghdad to deal in dates!'

'Was he trading dates in Cameroon as well?'

She gave me a look as if to say: now, don't be foolish.

'I don't know, why don't you write him a letter and ask for yourself. He doesn't like women meddling in his business affairs.'

'Where are you travelling to now, then?'

'To Berlin . . . both to visit the homeland and . . .' She ges-tured to the sallow-faced girl beside her. 'And for the child . . . she has a frail constitution so we brought her out with us for the winter. Now I am taking her home.'

'So you travel to Berlin often?'

'Twice a year.'

'So I take it that Herr Döppke's business affairs are going well?'

She smiled and wiggled flirtatiously.

Still I could not bring myself to ask. Now, I knew that my hesitation was not because I didn't know how to pose the ques-tion, but rather because I feared what I might learn. But was I not already resigned to my fate? I was drained of all passion. So why was I afraid? Maria might have found a Herr Döppke of her own. Perhaps she was still unmarried and racing from one man to the next, searching for the one she could believe in. Most likely she would not even recognize my face.

When I thought about it, I could not remember her face and for the first time in ten years I realized that neither of us had a photograph of the other . . . How shocking! Why hadn't we thought of that before parting? Yes, we'd believed that we would soon be reunited and yes, we trusted the power of mem-ory, but why had I not thought of this until now? Had I never felt the need to conjure up her face?

I remembered how I'd once known every line in her face – how during the first months I'd been able to conjure up that vision in a moment, without any difficulty whatsoever . . . Later . . . when I'd realized it was all over, I'd gone to great lengths to keep myself from seeing, or rather imagining, her. For I'd known I'd not be able to endure it. A single fleeting vision of the Madonna in a Fur Coat would have undone me.

Now my memories had lost their power to hurt me, but when I tried to cast my mind back, searching for her face, I found nothing . . . and I did not even have a picture of her . . .

Why would I need such a thing?

Glancing at her watch, Frau Döppke stood up. Together we walked to the station.

She was quite fond of Ankara and Turkey in general.

'I have never seen a country embrace foreigners so warmly. Think, for example, of Switzerland, a country that owes its well-being to all the foreigners passing through. People there look at foreigners as if they might burgle their homes . . . but here everyone seems eager to help a stranger in whatever way they can. And Ankara was truly lovely.'

The old woman was prattling on. The young girl was five or ten steps ahead of us, passing her hand over the trees lining the road. We were nearly at the station when at last I found my courage. Doing my best to feign indifference, I asked: 'Do you have many relatives in Berlin?'

'No, not many . . . I'm actually from Prague, a Czech German . . . My first husband was Dutch. Why do you ask?'

'It's just that during my time there I met a woman who told me that you were relatives . . .'

'Where?'

'In Berlin . . . We happened to meet at an exhibition. I think she was a painter . . .'

She was suddenly all ears. 'Yes . . . and then?'

Hesitating, I went on. 'And then . . . I don't know . . . we must have spoken just once . . . She had a beautiful painting . . . and that's how we . . .'

'Do you remember her name?'

'I think it must have been Maria Puder . . . That's it! Maria Puder! That was the name signed on the bottom of her painting. And in the catalogue . . .'

She did not answer. I mustered my courage again: 'Do you know her?'

'Yes, but how did she come to tell you that we were related?'

'I don't know . . . I suppose I told her about the *pension* and she must have said that she had a relative there . . . or was it something else . . . now I can't quite recall . . . it was ten years ago.'

'Yes . . . ten years is a long time . . . Her mother told me that she'd once had a Turkish friend and that she'd talked about him all the time and so I'm wondering if you are the very same person. But isn't it strange that her mother never once met this Turk that her daughter so admired . . . She'd gone to Prague that year and that's where her daughter told her that this Turkish student had left Berlin.'

We had arrived at the station. Frau Döppke was walking over to her train. I feared that if the topic of conversation changed I might not ever learn what I truly wanted to know. So I looked straight into her eyes to make clear my interest in hearing more.

After she dismissed the hotel attendant who had stowed her luggage in the train compartment, she turned to me and said: 'Why do you ask? You said you hardly knew Maria?'

'Yes . . . but she must have left a strong impression . . . I was very taken by her painting . . .'

'She was an excellent painter.'

With a sudden concern I could not understand, I asked: 'You said she *was* a good painter? Not now?'

She looked around for the young girl. Seeing that she had already climbed into the compartment and found her seat, Frau Döppke leaned closer: 'Obviously not . . . because she is no longer alive.'

'What?'

I heard the word whistle through my lips. People turned to look at us. The little girl stuck her head out of the window to watch me wide-eyed.

Frau Döppke gave me a long, searching look. 'Why such surprise?' she said. 'You look so pale. You said you didn't really know her.'

'Nevertheless. It's a shock to hear that she's died.'

'Yes . . . but not recently . . . it happened maybe ten years ago.'

'Ten years ago! Impossible . . .'

She gave me another searching look, and pulled me aside. 'Now I clearly see that you are intrigued by Maria Puder's death. So let me quickly give you the story. Two weeks after you left the *pension* to return to Turkey, Herr Döppke and I left as well and we went to visit relatives who had a farm on the outskirts of Prague. That's where we happened to see Maria and her mother. Now I don't get along well with her mother, but that's another matter. Maria was looking frail and wan, and she told us that she had suffered a grave illness in Berlin. Sometime later, mother and daughter went back to Berlin. Maria seemed to have recovered. By then we'd moved to East Prussia, my husband's homeland . . . When we returned to Berlin that winter, we heard that Maria had died at the beginning of October. Naturally I overlooked my disagreements with her mother and paid her a visit. She looked exhausted, like a sixty-year-old woman. Though she wouldn't have been more than forty, forty-five then. She told me that after they had left Prague Maria began to feel certain changes in her body and they went to the doctor who told them she was pregnant. Initially she was pleased, but despite her mother's entreaties she never told her who the father was. She always said that she would soon find out and she spoke of an imminent journey. In the final months of the pregnancy, her health took a turn for the worse and the doctors told her that she was at risk and that although it was late they wanted to intervene, but Maria would not allow that, and then suddenly she fell terribly ill and was taken to hospital. I suppose her albumin levels were very low . . . her body was only just recovering from everything she had gone through before . . . Even before she went into labour she lost consciousness several times. So the doctors did intervene and they managed to save the baby; but Maria continued to have seizures and one week later she passed away in a coma. She'd confided in no one. She never thought she was going to die. During her last moments of clarity, she told her mother how shocked she would be when she heard the whole story, but that in the end she too would rejoice. But she never gave her the father's name. Her mother remembered how her daughter often spoke of a Turk. But she had never met him, and didn't even know his name . . . The child was in and out of hospitals and nurseries until she was four, after which she went to live with her grandmother. She's a rather frail and quiet girl, but thoroughly charming . . . don't you think?'

I thought I might faint. My head was spinning, yet somehow I managed to keep standing and smiling.

'This girl?' I asked, nodding in the direction of the train window.

'Yes . . . she's sweet, isn't she? So quiet and well behaved! Who knows how much she misses her grandmother?'

She watched me carefully while she said all this. The glimmer in her eyes was almost hostile.

The train was about to leave. She climbed inside.

A little later the two of them appeared in the window. Smiling carelessly, the girl cast her eyes over the station, and occasionally she looked at me. The plump old woman beside her did not let me out of her sight.

The train lurched forward. I waved, as Frau Döppke threw me a final, vicious, smile.

She pulled the child inside . . .

All this took place just last night. Only twenty-four hours have passed since all this happened.

I did not sleep a wink last night. I just lay on my back, thinking of the child on the train. I could almost see her head, receding with the rattling train. And her hair . . . she'd had a good head of hair, but I could not recall what colour hair she had, or the colour of her eyes. I hadn't asked her name. I'd paid her no attention. Although at one point she had only been a step away from me, I'd not looked at her closely. When saying goodbye, I'd not taken her hand. And so I knew nothing – dear God – I knew absolutely nothing at all about my own daughter. No doubt Frau Döppke had sensed something . . . Why had she looked at me with such malice? No doubt she had made inferences . . . and then left with the girl . . . They are travelling now . . . the wheels of the train are rolling over the tracks, gently tossing my daughter in her sleep.

Every minute of the day, I chased after them in my thoughts. And at long last, just as I thought I could endure no more, the image I had driven from my mind began very slowly, and very quietly, to take shape before my eyes: Maria Puder, with her dark eyes and deep gaze and fine curving lips. My Madonna in a Fur Coat. There was not a trace of anger or ill will in her face. There was, perhaps, a note of surprise, but more than that, there was concern and compassion. Yet I did not have the courage to meet her gaze. For ten years – fully ten years – I had, in my wretchedness, loathed and condemned a dead woman . . .

could there be a greater insult to her memory? For ten years I had wrongly and unequivocally doubted the person who was my life, my soul, my reason for living, without once considering that I might be doing her an injustice. For all the garish scenarios I'd dreamt up, never once had I stopped and asked myself whether there might have been a good reason for her leaving me. And it turned out there had been a reason, the gravest, most immovable reason: death. I felt I might die of shame. I was wracked with despair and the needless remorse we feel in the face of death. If I were to spend the rest of my life in supplication, seeking forgiveness for having murdered her memory, I fear I would not succeed – for the greatest betrayal, the greatest sin we can commit against the most blameless, is to abandon a loving heart, and for that I shall never be forgiven.

Only a few hours ago I was under the impression that, lacking a picture, I would not be able to recall her face again.

Yet now I can see her, in all her beauteous detail, and she is more alive than she ever was in life. As in her self-portrait, she looks a little wistful and a little proud. Her face is a little paler, her eyes darker. She's pushed out her lower lip, as if to say, 'Oh Raif!' Yes, she is more alive than ever . . . So she died ten years ago! While I was waiting for her, getting our home ready for her. Without saying a word about me to anyone, so as not to cause me trouble. And then she'd died, taking her secret with her.

Now I understood the anger I'd felt for her over these ten years – and why I'd built an insurmountable wall between me and the world: for ten years I had carried on loving her, loving her with all my heart. That was why I had allowed no one else in. But now I loved her even more than ever before. Opening my arms to the vision that was Maria, I imagined taking her hands and rubbing them warm once more. I could see every detail of the months we had spent together: every moment shared and every word exchanged. Returning to that moment when I first saw her painting in the exhibition, I lived it all again: I listened to her singing at the Atlantic; and then she came and sat beside me. We visited the botanical gardens, and sat across from one another in a room, and then she fell ill. These memories were rich enough to fill an entire lifetime. Compressed into such a short space of time, they were all the greater and more vibrant than anything real could ever be. They showed me that I had not been truly alive for a single moment over the past ten years – my thoughts, feelings and actions had travelled far away from me, so far that they might as well have belonged to a stranger. I might be nearly thirty-five years of age, but the real me had only ever been alive during those four or five months ten years ago: since then I had been buried deep inside an alien shell, signifying nothing.

Last night in bed, when I came face to face with Maria, I understood how difficult it was going to be to carry on inside this body, this mind, that had nothing to do with me. When I ate, I would be feeding a stranger. I would drag myself from place to place, watching the world with a mixture of pity and scorn. Last night I came to understand that life held nothing more for me, now that she was dead: I had died with her, if not before.

Early this morning, the rest of the household went out on an excursion. Claiming to be unwell, I stayed at home. I have been writing since morning. Now night is falling. They have not come home yet. But soon the house will fill with their shouting and laughter. What does any of it mean to me? When all human ties are severed, what is left? I have not uttered a single true word in ten years. But now, how desperately I need a confidant. What else is there left for me, but to spill out these words and then drown in them? Oh, Maria, why can't we sit by the window and talk? Why can't we open our hearts and souls to each other, as we walk together in silence on a windy autumn evening? Oh, why aren't you here with me?

Perhaps I have needlessly shunned society for all these years. Perhaps, in refusing to believe them, I have treated people unfairly. Perhaps, had I looked, I might have found someone like you. Had I learned of your death sooner, I might have recovered in time to make the effort to find you in someone else. But it is all over now. Knowing the monumental and unforgivable injustice I have visited on my beloved, I lack the will to put things right. I have held the whole world in contempt, on account of having misjudged you; I have shut myself away. Now I can see the truth. All the same, I have no choice but to condemn myself to everlasting solitude. Life is a game that is only played once, and I lost. There is no second chance . . . My years ahead will be even worse than the years already past. I shall continue to go shopping every evening, like a machine. I shall meet and tolerate people in whom I have no interest. Could I have continued living in any other way? I think not. Had I been spared this chance encounter, I might have carried on living as before, oblivious to the truth. You were the one who taught me that another life was possible, and that I had a soul. And it is not your fault that it ended too soon . . . Thank you for giving me the chance to be truly alive. Those few months were worth a few lifetimes, don't you think? The child you have left behind, a part of you, our daughter – she will wander the far corners of this earth without knowing her father . . . Our paths crossed once. But I know nothing about her. Neither her name nor where she lives. But she will always be in my heart, and my mind. In my mind I shall imagine a life for her, and in that life I shall walk beside her. In my dreams I shall watch her growing up. I shall see her to school. I shall know her smiles and come to understand the way she thinks, and with all of this I shall try to fill the void ahead. I can hear noise outside. They must be back. But I want to keep writing. What is the point in that? I have written so much, and what of it? I shall have my daughter buy another notebook tomorrow and hide this one. I shall hide it all away, in a place no one will ever find. Everything, everything. But especially my soul.

Raif Efendi's notebook finished with those words. The notebook's remaining pages were blank. It was as if he'd taken the decision to release the soul he'd kept hidden so long and so fearfully, but after spilling it onto these pages, he'd sunk back into himself, never to speak again.

It was early in the morning by now. Keeping the promise I had made, I put the notebook in my pocket and I went to his house. The moment the door swung open, to wailing and confusion, I knew what had happened. For a moment I stood there, unsure of what to do. I did not want to leave without seeing Raif Efendi one last time. But after the night I had just spent with him, in love and truly alive, I could not bear the prospect of seeing him reduced to that empty vessel that signified nothing. I stepped back into the street. Raif Efendi's death did not overly distress me. For I felt that, rather than losing him, I had somehow found him.

Last night he'd said to me, 'We never got the chance to sit down and talk.' But now I knew differently. Last night we'd spoken for many long hours.

That same night, he'd left his life behind and entered mine. And there he would remain, truly alive – more so than anyone I'd ever known. Wherever I went, he'd be there at my side.

When I got to the office, I sat down at Raif Efendi's empty desk. Placing his black notebook before me, I turned back to the first page.

November 1940–February 1941